TO THE SIERRA MADRE

BUCKSKIN CHRONICLES BOOK 6

B.N. RUNDELL

WOLFPACK PUBLISHING
— EST 2013 —

Published in the United States by Wolfpack Publishing, Las Vegas.

Wolfpack Publishing
6032 Wheat Penny Avenue
Las Vegas, NV 89122

wolfpackpublishing.com

Library of Congress Control Number: 2018908734

Paperback ISBN: 978-1-62918-682-5
eBook ISBN: 978-1-62918-686-3

It's been a good ride. This is my eighth novel in less than a year. Considering I didn't start this ride until I was almost seventy-one years old, it has been absolutely amazing. I am grateful to my many readers that have waded through the countless words and found pleasure, encouragement, and even inspiration. That is very humbling to me as a writer, to know that words penned at my dining room table can circulate throughout the world and find a home on someone's nightstand or beside their easy chair and eventually into the minds and hearts of others. Thank you. And to the love of my life, without her this and any other work ever accomplished by me would not have been possible. Her support, inspiration, and encouragement give meaning to each and every day and purpose to my life. My wife, Dawn, has faithfully been by my side for over a half-century and she's planning on that much more. So, thank you, my beloved. And to my children and grandchildren who have repeatedly expressed their pride in this old man and have continually been a source of pride for me and mine.

TO THE SIERRA MADRE

A WINTER IN THE HIGH LONESOME WITHOUT preparation is an open invitation to a long and painful death. Many a tale has been told by the pioneers and trappers who explored the high country of friends found with icicles hanging from their beards with frozen hands clasped tightly to their weapons while sightless eyes stared at the endless ocean of white before them. Pilgrims that wander into the mountains thinking they can handle anything that comes their way soon find snow drifts anywhere from ten to thirty feet in depth. They foolishly try to make their horses, that have more sense than their riders, plough through the frozen crust on the snow to their own peril. Such fools should never be let out of the city and should stay where they can at least find shelter in some broken down shanty. There is no refuge for fools in the mountains.

Caleb led the way as he trailed the pack horse with the elk carcass tightly secured. Clancy followed on her long legged appaloosa mare that was a spitting image of the stallion under Caleb. He stopped and waited for Clancy to pull alongside as he rested his hands on the saddle horn and took in the view before him. In the midst of a grove of Aspen with the golden leaves quaking in the breeze, the white bark framed the view of the valley below them with the snow dusted mountains providing a backdrop of majesty outlined by the brilliant blue and cloudless sky. He took a deep breath, looked over at his redheaded freckle faced wife and said, "Have you ever seen anything as beautiful as that?" as he motioned with a nod of his head to the panorama before them. She smiled at the broad shouldered man astride his appaloosa stallion and remembered the first time she saw him almost a decade ago. A scared girl that was hiding out in the brush with her big black dog, Two Bits, after having witnessed the massacre of the small wagon train that she and her Mum and Da were traveling with through the Wind River Mountains. A Crow raiding party had killed everyone and now she saw another Indian with a white man and a boy about her own age. But she was fortunate to be taken in by the man, Jeremiah, and his wife, Laughing Waters that were the adopted parents of Caleb, the young man that was now her husband and father of the child they were expecting. Resting her hand on her belly, she thought of the child they lost at birth and how the grief drove them to flee the mountains in an effort to stifle that grief amidst the crowds of St. Louis. But the mountains called them back and now they were happily preparing for the first winter in their new home in the Medicine Bow Mountains. As she looked at the smile of contentment and joy that covered the face of her husband, she echoed his sentiments with, "Yes, I have. We have been blessed to see many vistas that compare with that one, in the Wind River Range, the Absaroka, and even the Big Horns. But each one is special, and this view is very special because this is ours!" She leaned over to meet him halfway for a kiss, his hand grasped her neck as he held her tightly against him and let their embrace linger.

As she pulled back to regain her balance, he said, "But I like this view the best," as he grinned at his redhead. She giggled and said, "Oh come on now Romeo, we've got to get this meat back to the cabin and put up. It's gonna take a good while to smoke all this." She whistled for her dog, Rowdy, the replacement for Two Bits, to follow and he obediently trotted alongside with his red tongue lolling to the side.

"Not if we have a couple of good steaks off it first! Course, the fellas might want a slice or two if they didn't get anything. Sometimes I think they just ride around lookin' at the country and don't know what to do when they see any elk or deer or anything. Heaven forbid they should run into a grizz or sumpin'." The men were the four that joined them when they split off from the trade caravan of buffalo hunters. Reuben, the big black stevedore they met on the docks at St. Louis and a man that handled horses and mules with a deft touch, Brewster, the young man from the stables that was a scrounger and hard worker, and the Threet brothers, Colton and Chance, who hired on as hunters but chose to leave with Caleb and Clancy for a life in the mountains.

Caleb had contracted with James Heffernan, the

brother of Margaret Heffernan Borland, a Texas widow rancher, to partner on starting a ranch in the Medicine Bow Valley. Caleb and company would establish the ranch and Heffernan would bring up a herd of about one thousand cattle in the spring for the start of one of the first ranches in the Rocky Mountains. Although Caleb and his company of recruits knew very little about cattle ranching, Heffernan promised to bring some experienced vaqueros and others to ensure things got off to a good start. But for now, the focus was on preparing for a winter in the mountains.

The short distance to their cabin was covered in just moments. It was a well built cabin with plank flooring made from the remains of a wagon train discovered in the foothills of the Medicine Bow Mountains. There were scant clues as to the consequence of the wagon train's departure from the usual route of the Oregon Trail and the eventual massacre, but it was a resource for much needed lumber and other items. The couple's cabin was a two room cozy home for Caleb and Clancy while the rest of the men had their own abode farther back into the timber. The setting, with enough of a clearing to provide room for corrals and sheds, was an idyllic location well protected by towering black timber yet providing a clear view of the valley below and the distant mountains of the Snowy Range.

Caleb led the pack horse to the edge of the clearing where a sturdy lodge-pole log hung suspended between two tall ponderosa. Dismounting, he tied a rope to the hind legs of the carcass throwing the loose end over the log and hoisted the hind quarter half of the elk to hang suspended well off the ground. He repeated the process for the front half of the carcass, tied off the ropes and led the pack horse to the corral. Clancy was busy removing the saddle and gear from her horse while Caleb's stallion patiently waited his turn to be unburdened and released into the corral. The horses knew they were home and there would be hay and a few oats waiting. After carrying their gear to the tack shed, the couple took a breather on their porch before starting the work of cutting up the carcass and smoking the meat to preserve it for the coming winter. The couple's relationship had evolved to that stage where constant conversation was unnecessary as the silent communication of like minds anticipated the actions and responses of the other. Now, seated together in silence, they clasped hands and leaned toward one another and savored the silent moment. While they enjoyed their respite, the mood was interrupted by the return of the men with a hail from Reuben, "Hey you two lovebirds! Don'tcha know you 'sposed to be out huntin' so we'uns can have sumpin' to eat come winter?"

Caleb smiled at the big man and nodded his head in the direction of the hanging carcass at the edge of the clearing. Reuben and the others looked at the meat and back at the couple and then together motioned to the two pack animals behind them. The two big mules were carrying the carcasses of two deer and a sizable black bear. Caleb was only able to tell the bear by a big paw and the black nose that barely protruded from under the canvas wrapped bundle. The mule carrying the bear carcass was still a bit skittish and begrudgingly followed the men under protest of its cargo. It was a natural self-preservation instinct of any animal that knew the bear was a predator and under usual circumstances they were the prey. It was obvious the mule was anxious to be rid of his pack and the smell of the bear, but Caleb and Clancy were glad to see the take of the men and especially the bear that would provide ample fat for cooking grease and a hide for warmth.

Many hands made light work and within a few hours strips of meat suspended on willow racks were being smoked over slow burning coals and Clancy was busy preparing biscuits and her well-received medley of Indian potatoes, onions and an unnamed mystery addition, she liked to keep her boys on their toes. She had several slices of elk steak skewered on the rotisserie bar over the fireplace fire and the dripping grease occasionally popped and sizzled a reminder to the cook. She enjoyed cooking for her boys, as she called the cadre of recruits, and they eagerly partook of her offerings, much preferring them to their own fare.

As the darkness made silhouettes of the surrounding trees against the moonlit sky, the men eagerly entered the cabin and took their place at the table. Clancy leaned back against her counter with arms folded across her chest as she smiled at the menagerie of men with their big appetites and grinning faces. It was a long standing rule they had to wash up and comb their hair before they would be allowed at her table and she was pleased to see the freshly groomed men standing behind the chairs and benches waiting for the woman of the house to take her place. They remained standing as Reuben took his turn at asking the Lord's blessing for their meal. He began, "Almighty God, we be thankin' you fo' all yo' blessin's, for the meat we gots today, the meal yo' provided us wit, and the family we be a part of, but we thanks you mostest fo' yo' Son and our Savior, da Lawd Jesus Christ. Thank you God, an' bless this food to our bodies. Amen." His words were echoed by everyone with a chorus of "Amen" and the benches and chairs scraped the floor as they seated themselves for the feast.

IT WAS AN UNUSUALLY DRY FALL SNOW WITH BIG flakes that drifted slowly down to disappear on the warm ground. Caleb sat on the split log bench on the porch remembering how his mother, Jeremiah's sister, in Michigan territory described this kind of snow. "The angels in Heaven are fluffing the clouds and the snowflakes are the feathers from the pillows of the angels." He smiled at the memory of the mother that tried to put a spiritual application to everything in life, but she had fallen silent when the epidemic of Typhoid took his father and would eventually take his mother. With a heavy sigh, he looked at the figure of his wife leaning against the door jamb and taking in the sight of the first fall snow. She sidled over to the bench and joined her husband. They both nourished steaming cups of coffee and savored the moment of togetherness. "It's beautiful, isn't it?" she observed.

"Yeah, I always like this kind of snow. It's sure beats that horizontal kind, that's for sure."

They silently reminisced of winters past and shared, sipped the hot java and leaned against one another. Suddenly Caleb stiffened and straightening up leaned forward for a better look. He turned to his wife to see if she was looking in the same direction, then turning back to peer through the white veil of winter, he watched as several horsemen walked their horses to the hot springs and the rising cloud of steam in the bottom of the valley. The snow was thick enough to obscure the view and prevent any recognition of the horsemen, but the way they rode and dismounted, Caleb was sure they were Indians. He stepped back into the cabin, secured his Sharps and a pocketful of paper cartridges and caps and returned to the porch. While Caleb watched the visitors, Clancy retrieved her Hawken, horn and possibles bag and rejoined her husband. "You watch them, I'm gonna fetch the men."

He quickly trotted to the men's cabin and stormed in, "Get your weapons! We might have visitors!" The men scurried in response to his alarm without asking needless questions and joined Caleb at the corner of the cabin. Caleb instructed the men to different observation points and cautioned them, "Hold your fire unless I give you a signal."

"What kind of signal?" asked Brewster, the youngest of the bunch.

"You'll know!" he hollered over his shoulder as he jogged back to his cabin.

At a glance he could see Clancy had loaded and primed her Hawken and he grinned at her readiness as she stood next to the porch post. He joined her and asked, "Can you make out who they are?"

"I'm sure they're Indian, but I don't know if they're Utes or not, I ain't never seen any Utes before."

Caleb cautiously stepped from the porch and using the large trunk of a big ponderosa at the edge of the clearing for cover, he moved closer to better observe the visitors. Although the snow continued, it was just enough to provide a bit of silent cover for his observation. He counted sixteen warriors but couldn't tell if any had paint on, but they all disrobed and waded into the hot springs and sat to soak. They were talking but Caleb could not hear the conversation but he gathered by their action this was not an unusual activity for them. This was their territory and it would certainly be plausible they would know of the existence and benefits of the hot mineral bath so Caleb was not alarmed they were here, but he was cautious. He looked back to the cabin to see if any smoke was coming from the chimney to betray their presence, but Clancy had let the fire from their morning meal and coffee die down and there was nothing more than a thin wisp of smoke that blended with the snowflakes. They purposely built the cabin to be obscured by the trees and terrain so it was not easily recognizable to anyone that did not know it was there. He looked back and watched the men laze around in the shallow pool of steamy water. Turning to motion to Clancy that the visitors were going to be a while, he saw Reuben join her at the porch. Caleb turned to watch the basking Indians and seated himself beside the tree.

After about a half hour, Caleb watched as the men

began exiting the steamy water and don their clothing and mount to leave. He knew he could not be seen by the party but he noticed one man pause, turn and look directly at Caleb, raise his arm and with open palm appeared to wave. After a moment of staring in the direction of the cabin, the man turned and followed his friends. Caleb stood, returned to the cabin and in response to Clancy's inquiry said, "Yeah, I'm sure they were Utes, but the darnedest thing happened, one o' them looked right thisaway and raised his hand and waved like he was sayin' goodbye or sumpin'."

"He couldn't see us, could he?" she asked with a touch of concern in her voice.

"Nah, I'm sure he couldn't, but he mighta already knowed we was here. Course, I'd be more surprised if they didn't know we were here, we haven't exactly tried to make a secret of it or anything."

"But you'd think they'd of done something, you know, visit or attack or at least show themselves," commented Clancy.

Both Reuben and Caleb nodded in agreement but had little more to offer. Looking at the snow, Reuben asked, "Ya think this be gonna 'mount ta' anything?"

"Nah, it's just an early fall storm," observed Caleb as he stretched out from under the porch roof and looked heavenward only to have several big flakes cause him to blink and retreat under the overhang. "These usually just last a day or so, don't normally amount to much. We'll still have time to fill the cache," he stated as he nodded toward the cache he and the men had built on four stilts behind the cabin. It was constructed in the same fashion as the cabin, only much smaller and high above the reach of any prowling predators and would be a secure place for their winter supply of meat. With most of the meat already taken smoked or cured into jerky or pemmican, the remainder of their meat would be stored in the cache and would be well kept with the temperatures lowering into the thirties and below.

"But you know, Reuben, I'm thinking our next few outings for meat, we need to be extra careful of the Utes, we still don't know for sure if they're aware of us, but we sure need to be aware of them. And if you see any sign of their village, you know, trails leading somewhere you haven't been, smoke, anything that might give you an idea. Be sure to steer clear and no shootin' or anything that might give you away."

"Don't you think I know dat?" asked the grinning Reuben as he leaned against the porch post. "Just cuz you found me in St. Louie don't mean I don't know nuthin' 'bout the woods and Indians and such." Reuben had already proven himself a good woodsman and hunter as well as a substitute father to the other three but Caleb felt compelled to offer the words of caution anyway.

"I know that, but I've lived with Indians and I know a little bit more how they think and act. Course, just like anybody else, there's good un's and bad un's, but people that have lived their entire lives in the mountains think a bit different than what you might be used to and it always pays to be cautious."

"I unnerstand, and we'll always be extra cautious," replied Reuben as he stepped down from the porch. "I think I'll roust the rest of them fellas out and see if'n we cain't get some more meat. I'm thinkin' 'bout tryin' to cross oe'r that saddle back yonder between them two smaller peaks an' see what's on the other side, might be some new country yonder."

"Well, we're gonna stay this side o' the creek an' check out this timber behind us again. Be careful o' them Grizzlies, they ain't very agreeable this time of year," cautioned Caleb as Reuben waved over his shoulder.

Clancy had overheard the conversation between Reuben and her husband and had already started preparing for another hunting trip before Caleb stepped back into the cabin. Leaning against the wall next to the door was their hunting gear to include saddle bags, her Hawken and powder horn and possibles bag, a small parfleche that he knew would contain provisions for the day and other necessities. Lying across the top of the pile were two partially beaded buckskin coats with warm rabbit fur linings. These were not their heavy winter robes but would be more than comfortable for this days outing. He smiled up at his wife as she stood in her familiar place and stance with arms folded across her chest and a smile on her face and the dog at her feet as she asked, "Is there anything else we'll need?" He knew she had forgotten nothing and he just shook his head as he stepped in front of her and took her in his arms in a welcome and lingering embrace. The dog moved aside for the lovers and flopped back down near the door. Caleb looked at him and thought how he was becoming another Two Bits, the childhood companion of Clancy that was left behind with their parents when they made the trip to St. Louis. It was the first time Clancy had been without her pet, but she knew he was getting too old to for that kind of travel. His muzzle was already showing the white hairs of age and his gait had slowed considerably, but he would still be a good companion for Laughing Waters, their adopted mother and Shaman of the Arapaho, on her many journeys alone. Now Rowdy, the pup Clancy adopted in St. Louis from the DuBois family, was growing to the size of Two Bits, who was often thought to be a bear because of his size and thick coat. Rowdy, just like Two Bits, would not let Clancy out of his sight and had already shown his protective nature toward his mistress. Now he would join them on their foray into the timber on another hunting trip.

THE SNOW CONTINUED TO DRIFT LAZILY DOWN IN typical fall fashion. The hats and coats of the hunters briefly held the big flakes that took temporary hold on the four figures that trailed single file across the wide valley. Scattered clumps of sage looked like frosty humps of white buffalo and the random patches of cactus impaled the large flakes to keep them suspended in space before the weight of their companions dropped them to the valley floor to disappear among the warm rocks and clay soil. It was the type of scene best enjoyed from the warmth of a cabin while seated before a fireplace with a window to oversee the wintry landscape. But these men were on a mission for meat. Although inexperienced with the subtleties and nuances of hunting big game in the mountains, they were learning in the unforgiving school of experience. Led by the big man, a former stevedore on the docks of St. Louis, Reuben, the band of four hunters followed single file with shoulders hunched and hats pulled low to keep the cold initiating snow from necks and face. While the three young men tried in vain to hunker deeper in their saddles, the single sentinel of danger was their leader.

Looming in the distance some five or six miles away was the saddle between the larger tree covered knobs that was their goal. The snow sought to obscure the view, but like the child's toy known as a jack-in-a-box, the saddle would appear and disappear behind the white curtain at uneven intervals. Their nearer goal was the tree-line at the edge of the valley where they would take their noon-ing. The frosted black timber raised their heaven pointing needle tops as a beacon to the wanderers and Reuben's shoulders dropped in relief as he anticipated the shelter and fire with a coffee pot of warming brew. The broad shoulders and hulking figure of the big man turned to signal his followers that their noon camp was near. They rode into the shelter of the black timber and within a short distance came to a slight clearing that would afford shelter for the men and graze for the horses, whose manes and tails showed snow melted into icicles. It was a cold morning and the sun had yet to make it clear of the grey clouds in the East. Stepping down from their mounts, the young men were quick to gather armloads of firewood for a fire while Reuben readied the coffeepot filling it from his canteen.

Seated around the fire and waiting for the slow brewing coffee, the four men stared into the flames trying to draw the warmth to their lean frames. The youngest, Brewster, with his dirty blonde hair that sought escape from his floppy felt hat and his peach fuzz whiskers at his chin, showed his youth and inexperience from behind his arms folded over his broadening chest. The Threet brothers, Chance and Colton were seated side by side on a grey log and held their hands toward the flames as they looked with sightless eyes from thought filled minds as they appeared to be deep in silent conversation with one another. While Brewster was a curious and impulsive young man, the brothers were insightful and deliberate. The brothers had lean frames, light brown hair and handsome faces and could have passed for twins, but the younger, Colton, was slightly shorter than his older brother, Chance, who stood just shy of six feet. Both boys were quick of mind and fast of reflex with an agility that would make a cougar jealous. Although Brewster was the youngest of the three, he was maturing physically into a solid frame with broad shoulders and a developing strength that served him well in these wild mountains and the life he sought with this unusual assortment of would-be mountain men.

"So, Reuben, it looks like the snow's lettin' up a little, what's your plan?" asked Brewster.

The big black man looked at the youngster and in his thunder rumbling voice replied, "The way I figger it, them elk'll hunker down in the timber 'till the sun comes out, 'n then'll take their time movin' out an' about. That'll give us time to work up this saddle a mite, look the country o'er an' then we can spread out an' push thru the timber. Caleb says it's a good move to put a couple on points that the elk might break out and the rest of us push our way thru to kick 'em out and mebbe get a shot at some o' 'em." As he finished explaining the plan, he reached for the pot, poured a little cold water into it to settle the grounds and sat it back down on the flat rock at the edge of the fire. Each man produced his cup and waited their turn for the warm java. The leader of the crew was the biggest as well. Standing about six feet three inches and easily weighing in about two hundred fifty or more, he was all muscle. His reputation on the riverfront was as the strongest man on the levee and not one to get riled. When seen without a shirt, the muscles fought for attention with the shoulders and upper arms bulging like massive black boulders that sat on a black marble torso that tapered to narrow hips. Although soft-spoken and even tempered, the flashes from his dark brown eyes that stared from under the protruding brow told the viewer to beware the power that resided within. He looked around at the young men of his charge and smiled at their enthusiasm and eagerness to grab life and wrestle it into submission. Yet he knew that they had much to learn about life in general as he had much to learn about life in the mountains. They were all students of the Medicine Bow.

As the men sipped the last of the rejuvenating brew, the sun made its appearance over the tree tops and lit the small clearing with long rays of light that were filtered through the last of the lazy drifting flakes of the season's first snow. Reuben looked up and let the sun warm his face and with eyes closed said, "Well fellas, looks like we're gonna have a day of huntin' after all." He stood and kicked dirt onto the remaining coals and turned to replace the coffee pot in the mule's pack. "We'll go together up the trail yonder and pick out some likely places to park a shooter, then we'll start the drive."

Knowing the daylight would slip away sooner than planned, the men again moved out single file with Reuben in the lead. Cresting a slight rise in the trail, the way before them opened into a well lit park that showed sign of a recent elk herd. Reuben reined up and shaded his eyes as he looked at what appeared to be the trail of a herd that was moving down the hillside into the thicker timber. The men now rode with their rifles across the pommels of their saddles, ready for the first sight of any game. The strewn boulders, scrub oak and chokecherry, on the sloping hillside offered little cover for a herd of elk yet afforded a view of the downhill side that would give the animals warning when they rested in the open spaces. Reuben put heels to his mount as the hunters started to cross the clearing. Suddenly the big bay dropped out from under Reuben at the same time he heard the explosion of the rifle uphill from him. Tumbling end over end he held tightly to his Hawken as his shoulder hit the dirt below the scrub oak brush. The other men shouted and vaulted from their saddles to seek cover, Chance staggered as another rifle sounded from the trees. Reuben spotted the smoke from the attacker's rifle and took bead on the spot, with a quick set of his rear trigger, he lined out his shot through the buckhorn sight and the bronze blade of his front sight, squeezed off his shot and was rewarded with a scream from the assailant. He turned to see to his men and noted Chance lying unconscious but protected behind a sizable boulder, Colton was by his side and knelt with his rifle resting on the stone. Brewster had skittered behind the far side of the same cluster of scrub oak that shielded Reuben and he whispered, "Is it Injuns?"

"Don't know, but I think I winged one of 'em," said Reuben as he finished reloading his Hawken. Caleb had outfitted all the men with Hawken rifles when they stopped in Independence at the American Fur Company warehouse. The limited practice they had during the remainder of the trip West was sufficient to make each one proficient with the weapons. The Threet brothers had proven themselves to be excellent marksmen, but Chance was out of the fight. Reuben's quick glance at the brothers told him Chance was still breathing but his head was bloody, probably from a close graze that parted his hair. Reuben returned his gaze to search the tree line for any movement from their attackers. Colton spoke just loud enough to be heard by Reuben, "That big tall Ponderosa with the thick trunk is hidin' one of 'em. I'll chip some bark on the right side, you be ready for him to move to the left." Reuben nodded his head in under-standing and brought his sight to bear on the left side, about chest high. He nodded to Colton and waited. The thunder from Colton's Hawken expelled a cloud of grey white smoke and the bullet peeled bark from the tree. Reuben spotted a shoulder of buckskin and quickly squeezed off his shot and was once again rewarded with an outburst of pain from an attacker. The flurry of move-ment among the trees was insufficient to give a target but it was evident the attackers were fleeing. Soon the muted clatter of hoof beats was heard as horses carried the would-be assassins away.

Cautious of a trap from another assailant, the hunters stayed behind cover for a spell and the silence gave reason for Reuben to scurry to the side of the downed brother. Seating himself beside the brother, Reuben lifted Chance's head to his knee to examine the wound. As he thought, the boy would have an unplanned part to his hair, but he would recover. Taking a rag from his pouch and soaking it in water he cleaned the wound as Chance grimaced and looked up at his big nurse and asked, "Didja get 'em?"

"Well, we run 'em off, sure 'nuff," answered Reuben as Chance struggled to sit up. The sudden move brought pain to his head and he ducked as if someone hit him, grabbed his head and said, "Ow, that smarts!"

"Yeah, and it will for a spell, but you'll heal up, I reckon," then looking at the other two men, he said, "Let's gather up the animals and head on back to the cabin. Any elk or deer that was here probably headed to high country with all the shootin' an' I ain't sure those attackers are gone."

Reuben's bay was dead and sprawled a short distance away. The big man looked at his faithful mount, shook his head and began pulling his gear from the animal. Looking around, he told the others, "Put all dem packs on the smaller mule thar, I'se gonna ride da other'n."

As the men followed the trail from the saddle to the valley floor, Colton moved up alongside Reuben and asked, "Do you know who attacked us?"

"Not sure, but I don't think it was injuns," replied

Reuben. Colton looked askance at the big man, shook his head and said, "I think it was Bear and Catman, you know, those two trouble makers that Caleb kicked off the brigade back in Independence."

Reuben looked with a furrowed brow at Colton and asked, "What makes you think that?"

"I'm pretty sure the first one you hit, when he screamed and pulled back, was Catman. Remember that tripod thing he had on his rifle? I think I saw that when he jumped back."

"Could be, the other'n was big 'nuff to be his partner, Bear. Mebbe so," pondered Reuben. Again Colton looked at Reuben and spoke his mind, "Reuben, why is it sometimes you talk like you've been nothin' but a slave or whatever, then the next time it's like you've had more schoolin' than I have?"

The big man grinned and chuckled with a rumble in his chest and answered, "Well, back in St. Louie there was a Reverend that started a school for black folk. But St. Louie had a law against teaching black folk to read and write, so he moved the school out on one o' dem islands in the Mississippi River and set up out there. We'uns would make rafts or use boats and paddle out there of a night and learn. He was a good man and lots of us learned to read and write. I always enjoyed readin' and ever' chance I got, I would read anything I could find, newspapers, books anything. So, I learned to talk more like an educated man, but a lot of white folk don't like a black man bein' educated, thinks they get uppity an' such, so I have to act like I ain't got no learnin' sometimes."

Colton shook his head and said, "That ought not to be like that, but I understand what you mean. Chance and I have a few books we'll share with you, if you like."

"I'd like that a lot," replied Reuben with a broad smile and a nod of his head.

THE SUN HAD JUST TUCKED ITSELF AWAY BEHIND THE saddle notch of the timbered mountains to the West as Reuben and company reined up in the cabin's clearing to the welcome of Caleb and Clancy. In their customary place on the porch as the day bid adieu, they greeted the returning hunters with somber expressions that reflected the mood of the men. As the four dismounted, Caleb said, "No luck, eh? I thought sure you'd be bringin' home lots of meat, but I see you're a mite short on horseflesh. Run into some trouble didja?" It was then that Caleb noticed the bandage on Chance's head and turned to see if Clancy had spotted the bloody bandage. She had and was already on her way to the boy's side to examine the wound.

"You might say that," replied Reuben as he continued, ". . . ran into a bit of an ambush from a couple your old friends."

"Whaaat? Who?" queried Caleb with a startled look on his face as he jumped to his feet.

Reuben tossed the reins of the mule to Brewster and motioned for the boys to put the animals away as he walked to the porch to share the details. Clancy had already escorted Chance into the cabin for her to assess his wound. "Remember those two stinkin' idjits that you dumped back in Independence?"

"You mean Bear and Catman, the big bully and his sidekick with the knives?"

"That's them, we're purty sure they was the ones that ambushed us up on that saddle yonder. Lucky for us we had some cover and I think we mighta winged 'em both. But they lit outta there like a mad Grizzly was on their trail and we didn't foller 'em."

Caleb dropped his eyes to the steps, turned around and dropped on the bench and motioned for Reuben to have a seat as he pondered the revelation. With elbows on his knees he looked back at his friend, "I thought sure that ol' Beckwourth woulda taken those two and taught 'em a thing or two like he said but I reckon he just give 'em the boot like we did. You think they'll be followin' you?"

"Hard to say, but they was lyin' in wait fo us like they know'd we'd be comin', so I'm thinkin' they been hangin' 'roundchere fo a spell."

Caleb stood and paced the porch as he thought with occasional glances to the edge of the clearing and back to Reuben. He returned to his seat and looked to Reuben as he started, "Well, I'd say we need to take the fight to them, but with their trail bein' so far away I don't think that'd be a good idea. So, here's what I'm thinkin'. We'll stick close to home and prepare ourselves for their attack.

With Bear always tryin' to bully his way and countin' on his bulk, since he's lackin' a mite with brains, and with the two of 'em bein' so blasted sneaky and cowardly, I'm thinkin' they'd try their tricks at night. But we can't count on that, so we need to set a schedule of bein' on watch and always changin' things up."

The two men continued to hash out the possibilities and plan while the others put away the animals and gear and Clancy finished her preparations for supper. Caleb and Reuben shared the plans with everyone at the supper table and cautioned each one to never be caught alone. "And always be armed! It'd be best if you always had a handgun with you and more if possible, and it's best to be together no matter what you're doin'. An' if'n you see somethin', even if you don't know what it is, give the alarm with the call of a magpie." He demonstrated the yak, yak, yak cry of the scavenger black and white bird of the mountains and instructed each one as they tried to mimic the cry. After a few tries, each one was able to satisfactorily duplicate the bird's cry. Caleb was known as He Who Talks With the Wind among the Arapaho people for his uncanny ability to mimic the cries and sounds of every animal and bird he ever encountered. It was a talent that had often served him well when hunting prey, both the four legged and two legged variety. Now he hoped this would help protect those that were important to him.

Knowing that Clancy was more than likely the primary target of the attackers, Caleb refused her argument that she should take a turn on watch. "Babe, you know as well as I do that ugly stinkin' monster out there probably wants to even the score after you showed him up on the trip with the brigade. When you threw that knife and buried it in the log between his legs and scared him so badly, the men of the brigade laughed about that for days and he fumed about it all that time. Then after we forced him and Catman into the river at gunpoint so they'd take a bath, that made 'em madder'n a wet hornet and I'm sure they ain't forgot about it. So, they both wanna even the score and we ain't takin' no chances. Now, don't even step outta this house without havin' both that Navy Colt and me with you, understand?"

She stood with hands on hips and red rising into her cheeks as she said, "I can take care of myself! I showed that to them louts before an' I can do it again!"

"And you might get your chance, but I don't want any of us, you included, to go anywhere without company! And if you try it, I'll have to take you over my knee and spank some sense into you!"

His tense expression slowly turned into a grin as she said, "Does that mean I get to give you a spanking if you step outta line?" The rest of the men hooted and laughed at the stuttering response of Caleb as his face showed his perplexity with a bit of color.

"Whoooeee, Momma C, I'd sure like to see that!" exclaimed Colton using the pet nick name the boys had started using for their protective mother hen. The laughter had lightened the mood of the cabin as everyone resumed their seats at the table and shared their thoughts and additions to the plan of protection. As the men left the main cabin for their own retreat a short distance away, all were feeling confident with their preparations.

The second morning after their plan was in place, Caleb greeted the day standing in his doorway with a cup of steaming coffee in his hand. Somewhere farther upstream in the valley came the bugle of a big bull elk challenging all comers to test their mettle. He was probably the big bull of the woods and had already begun assembling his harem and dared any other bull to contest his will. Caleb grinned as he pictured the battle between two royal bulls as they tore up the turf and marked one another with the tines of their antlers. Having witnessed a bout between two denizens of the forest he knew it would be a battle to behold. Clancy saw the expression on his face and asked, "And just what has you taking a mind trip so early in the morning?"

"Didn't you hear it? That big ol' bull was challenging the youngsters to take him on."

She smiled as she walked to her husband's side and said, "The bugle of the bulls is a sure sign of the end of summer. They'll be roundin' up their harems and migrating to their winter range. I imagine we'll see some of 'em down in the valley yonder."

"Makes me wonder about the wisdom of bringin' in a bunch of cattle, they'll probably crowd all the elk out," he pondered as he thought of the plans made of establishing a cattle ranch in the valley. The Cherokee trail that connected the Sante Fe Trail and the Oregon Trail had already brought plenty of wagon trains through their valley and he wondered just how long this area would be free of pilgrims and settlers. Although plentiful with game now, the presence of people and cattle would alter those numbers considerably.

"Oh, I don't know. It seems to be the nature of things to change and adjust no matter what life brings. The animals have plenty of ways to ensure their survival, what with goin' to the high country in the summer when all the pilgrims come through and such. Besides, you're the one that's always tellin' me about how God is always in control. Don't you think He knows what's happenin' down here?"

"Yeah, you're right, as usual," he grumbled.

"Wait, say that again, I think I like the sound of that!" she joshed.

He grabbed her around the waist and pulled her close as he started tickling her sides to elicit a round of giggles from his mischievous wife. Then he pulled her up close and smothered her with kisses which she did not resist.

The rest of the day passed without incident. Reuben, Colton and Brewster made a quick trip upstream in the valley and brought home a good sized cow elk. Chance remained in the cabin recuperating from his head wound but Caleb, Clancy and Chance all welcomed the three hunters back into the glade. They made short work of quartering the elk and putting the meat in the cache and rolled up the salted hide to be worked at a later time. With the coming darkness, they again gathered in the main cabin for supper and enjoyed the time together as they partook of fresh elk steak, vegetables, and cornbread. Pushing back from the table Brewster said, "Momma C, you've done it again. That was a scrumptious meal."

Clancy grinned her appreciation and began the task of clearing the table but was quickly joined by the brothers and Brewster in her efforts. The supper chores done, the men retired to their cabin and the duties of the night. This night called for Brewster and Colton on watch first followed by Reuben and Chance with Caleb taking the early morning turn. They knew the most likely time any attack might come would be the early morning just as first light gave visibility. Reuben and Caleb knew they would probably be awake most of the night but might catch up on any lost sleep during the morning hours. For whatever reason, both the men were feeling uneasy as the stars chased the moon across the sky.

THE NIGHT SOUNDS TOLD OF A PEACEFUL TIME IN these early morning hours before daybreak. The stars shone with the usual brilliance that beckoned all creatures to look heavenward at the glories of God's marvelous creation. Caleb always enjoyed scanning the night sky and taking in the beauty of the Milky Way that spread like a broad diaphanous ribbon across the night. He would often search for the constellation Orion knowing that he and Clancy had chosen the lone star at the tip of the hunter's sword as their star, chosen so long ago during their youthful courtship in the distant mountains. He listened to the crickets, the recurring question from the nearby owl, and the bullfrog from the narrow ribbon of stream trickling through the nearby woods. He heard the muted chatter of a squirrel that sought its mate and the stealthy movement of a cautious deer as it tiptoed through the pine needles. He was leaning against a large twisted fir that hid his shadow as he watched the horses in the corral across the clearing. With heads hanging and standing hipshot, there was no sense of alarm among them. He scanned the tree line that was made visible with the starlight and the contribution of the last quarter of moon. There was nothing that told of any visitors.

Moving nothing but his eyes, he surveyed the entire clearing and anything he could see beyond but he detected no movement. Then he realized the bullfrog had gone silent, then the crickets retired their song, the stealthy deer had apparently spooked and bounced almost silently away. Caleb tensed and looked at the horses, now standing tall and with ears pricked forward they were looking into the shadows on the downhill side of the trees. Caleb turned toward the men's cabin and sounded the clear call of the magpie with a repeated yak, yak, yak, and again. Whatever or whoever was moving froze at the sound. Caleb did not move for he knew his call was an exact replica of the magpie and no one could tell the difference. With no other movement to alarm the intruders, they took a few cautious steps nearer and Caleb recognized the black shadows of the big man called Bear and the scrawny rat that followed him known as Catman. The big man was approaching the steps to the porch of the main cabin, moving with surprising stealth for a large and lumbering man, but just as his foot touched the first stone step he was stopped by the voice of Caleb coming from the darkness, "That's far enough!" He froze in place and turning just his head searched for the source of the warning, he let a frustrated growl escape, "How ya gonna stop me you little runt?"

"I don't need to stop you Bear, you can go 'head on an' open the door. There's a double barreled shotgun with hair triggers waitin' for you, so feel free," answered Caleb from the darkness. He moved after he spoke so his voice wouldn't present a target for the attackers. Bear looked at the door, stepped back and whispered at his accomplice, "Let's rush him, he can't get us both!"

Caleb suspected the two of some stupid response, but when the whisper set the two in motion, he was surprised at the attack of Catman and the flight of Bear. The wiry little man started to charge with a blast from his rifle toward the last location of the sound of Caleb's voice. Dropping his rifle and pulling a pistol from his belt and waving a knife with his other hand, he screamed as he charged but within a short distance from the tree line he triggered a well placed snare and was snatched from his feet and found himself hanging from one leg over eight feet from the ground. The snare was one of several traps set for any intruders since the ambush of the two attackers in the mountains. The trap caused him to drop his weapons and he now squealed at his partner, "Help! Help me! They got me hangin' from a tree!"

The cowardly bully used the charge of his partner to try to make good his escape, but he ran into the arms of Reuben that stopped him like a stone wall. When he bounced off the big black man with the help of a double handed push of a rifle across his chest, the surprised monster found himself on his back with his rifle out of reach in the darkness. He looked up to see what stopped his flight and heard the thunderous warning of Reuben, "If you're smart, you'll stay right where you are." But Bear was not known for his smarts and rolled to his hands and knees and showing surprising agility for a big man as he quickly put his feet under him and stood to a crouching stance as he whirled around to face the voice in the darkness. The blade of his knife gleamed in the moonlight and he snarled, "Come on whoever you are and I'll gut you like I planned. You must be that Nigra we saw in the mountain. I been wantin' 'nother chance atchu. This time I'll drop you like I did yore horse!"

With the big knife held lightly in his right hand, Bear began to move it side to side as he slowly advanced in his crouch searching for his victim. Reuben stood steady with his Hawken cradled before him as he considered just blowing a hole in the monster or taking him on in hand to hand combat. Setting his rifle against the nearby tree trunk, he stepped lightly into the deeper shadows and disappeared in the darkness. As Bear moved to where he thought Reuben stood, he was startled when the black man spoke from his right just above a whisper and asked, "Where ya goin' Bear, I ain't over there, lookee here." Yet as he spoke he moved quietly the opposite direction and when Bear growled, "Hold still Nigra, cuz I'm gonna peel yore hide like skinnin' a beaver."

"How ya gonna do that, you cain't even find me," chuckled Reuben from the other side of the man. Bear whirled to his left and lunged at what he thought was the big stevedore only to find his target to be nothing more than a snag of a tree. From the darkness behind him came a "Hee, hee, hee, whatsamatta Bear, think that there tree's gonna getchu?" The black man moved as quiet as a cougar and was showing himself to be even more deadly. He knew this was not a game and that death could easily be the final score, yet he wanted to taunt and confuse the mountain of a man that thought himself to be the king of the woods.

"I'm gettin' tired of waitin' on you Bear, I think I'm just gonna kill you like your namesake would, you know, maybe a good ol' bearhug," hissed Reuben from behind Bear. The grey light of early morning was cresting the Eastern horizon and the long shadows of the towering timber stretched across the glade with the pale light. Reuben hid behind the ragged stump of a fallen timber and cast his voice into the thicker woods confusing his adversary. On the other side of the clearing came the high pitched screaming of Catman still hanging from the Aspen with his buckskin coat tangling with his arms. Caleb had moved closer to the clash between the two behemoths to lend any aid necessary, but he knew Reuben harbored a grudge against Bear not just from the recent scrape, but because of Bear's bullying on the trip with the brigade. Reuben had tolerated the berating and name-calling with gritted teeth and taut muscles only to keep peace under the direction of the leader, Caleb. Now was his time to balance the scales. "Whatsamatta Bear, cat gotchur tongue? Where's those smart remarks? Gettin' sceared are ya'?" taunted Reuben as he continued to circle the confused and nervous Bear. Reuben knew the more frustrated and agitated Bear became, the more likely he would be to make a mistake. Boldly Reuben stepped from behind the tree and the growing light from his back cast a long shadow toward Bear. Reuben grinned and again taunted the rattled Bear. "Are you just gonna keep growling or are you gonna try to kill me?"

With a roar that rattled the long needles of the

towering ponderosa, Bear charged with his knife outstretched seeking the object of his derision. The ground was littered with cast off branches, pine cones and upthrust stones and his footing was unsteady but he lumbered on in his rage. At the last moment and without moving his feet, Reuben deftly twisted his torso just enough for Bear to miss his mark and the knife almost caught the corner of his buckskin tunic. But Reuben anticipated the move and with lightning quick reflexes dropped his open hand on the wrist of Bear and brought his other hand to the bottom of the wrist. Now with both hands wrapped around Bear's wrist, Reuben brought his arm straight up and with his massive thumbs on the back of Bear's hand, he swiftly brought his arm straight down resulting in the snap of Bear's arm with the crack of a pistol shot. The scream from Bear at the breaking of his arm rivaled the screams that came from his partner, Catman. Bear went to his knees as Reuben released his hold and stepped behind the man as Bear was on his knees and bending over holding his broken arm. With a hiss and a curse, he struggled to his feet and searched the ground for a weapon.

Spotting a large dead limb greyed by the weather, he covered the space in two large steps, grabbed a sizable limb and broke it off with another roar and turned to find Reuben. The clearing was empty and the big man spun side to side searching for his intended victim. With his broken right arm hanging to his side he growled, "Where are you Nigra? I'm gonna beatchur brains out!" Suddenly from behind him, arms slipped under his arm pits and hand clasped together behind his head as he was caught in the steely grasp of Reuben. The stevedore's voice thundered in his ears and asked, "Just how do you think you're gonna be doin' that?" Then with a grunt, Reuben leaned back and lifted Bear off his feet and with a heave befitting the man that could singlehandedly lift a bale of cotton he brought the man straight down to the ground and with the combined force of Bear's weight and the strength of Reuben, the snap of the backbone of Bear could be heard like another pistol shot. Bear landed in a heap, unable to move and with his weight against him he was unable to breathe and as Reuben stepped away, Bear's eyes closed in death.

Suddenly an explosion came from the porch of the cabin as Clancy's Hawken launched a missile of death at the running figure of Catman. He had cut himself free with one of his many harbored knives and was now charging the back of Caleb who was frozen in place as he witnessed the death of Bear. But the impact of the .54 caliber lead from the Hawken lifted him off his feet and threw his body several feet to land in a heap on his side. Blood began to pool beneath his lifeless body as Caleb approached with his rifle at the ready. He looked back at the porch and saw Clancy busily reloading her rifle to be ready for any other threats to their homestead.

She looked up at Caleb and over at Reuben as they both stood staring at the pregnant woman on the porch. The three younger men came trotting around the corner of the house and with a quick look at the crumpled bodies of the attackers, they too looked at Clancy. She grinned at her audience and said, "Ain't nobody gonna stab my man in the back!"

THE JACKRABBIT TOOK SEVERAL HOPS ON HIS BIG snowshoe feet with his long ears laid back and almost touching his tail and stopped. Coming erect, he looked across the glistening snow and listened, turning his head in short jerky movements he surveyed the sloping hillside that ended in the valley bottom at the slight indentation that showed the path of the frozen over stream that trickled silently under the deep ice and snow. With the sun blazing down from a cloudless blue sky the sparkles that twinkled from the pristine white blanket spoke of the temperatures that hovered around zero. The rabbit started to reach for the snow with his front paws when a shadow from behind became the swooping snatch of eagle's talons that carried away the white screaming rabbit leaving a trail that ended abruptly without expla-nation. The unfolding drama was witnessed by the lounging bundle of black fur that sat at the feet of Clancy on the porch of the cabin. With his head raised and ears cocked his eyes trailed the disappearing eagle across the azure panorama. Dropping his chin to his outstretched legs he made a feeble attempt at wagging his tail as Clancy dropped her hand to stroke his fur.

"Sure glad that wasn't you out there Rowdy, aren't you?" He lifted his head to look at his mistress and let his tongue fall from his open mouth as he smiled at her expecting more petting.

"Who you talkin' to?" asked Caleb as he stepped onto the porch carrying a steaming hot cup of fresh coffee.

"Oh, me'n Rowdy were just discussing the ways of life and death in the wilderness," drolly replied Clancy.

"And did you solve the problems of the world in this deep discussion?"

"Sure did, didn't we boy?" stated Clancy as she leaned down to stroke her companion.

Caleb seated himself beside his wife and looked through the trees to the valley below and smiled as he enjoyed the beauty of winter. The fir and spruce were heavily laden with the recent wet snow that threatened to break branches and the big pines held the white blankets as offerings to the gods of winter. Nothing had been disturbed by wind or creature and the only tracks were those left by the ill-fated journey of the big jackrabbit. The chilly temperature was held at bay by the couple as they cuddled under the heavy buffalo robe and sipped the black brew. Caleb put his arm around Clancy and rested his hand on her growing tummy and she smiled back at her husband and said, "I'm thinkin' it's gonna be a boy."

Caleb flashed a grin and replied, "I'm just tryin' to figger out how we can keep whatever it is from havin' red hair and freckles!" Clancy elbowed him in the ribs and said, "Only a few of God's chosen people get blessed with those traits. My Mum used to say our freckles were from the times the angels kissed us, too bad the angels didn't wanna kiss you!" He pulled her back closer to him as they enjoyed the moment of the morning.

The accumulating snow had now buried the lower limbs of the trees at the edge of the clearing and had Caleb not shoveled it off the porch, they would have had a difficult time getting out of the cabin. The hip high rail across the front of the porch now nestled just below the level of the snow. The cleared path away from the porch was beginning to resemble the canyons carved by rivers through the gorges of the mountains. When Caleb would go to tend to the animals the snowbanks were as high as his armpits. From a distance, the cabin was barely visible as the drifts nearby reached depths of well in excess of ten feet. This was proving to be an exceptionally harsh winter.

Although Clancy was enjoying the snuggling, she pulled away from Caleb and turned so she could look directly at him as she asked, "Uh, I've noticed you seem to be troubled about something, what is it?"

With a deep breath and a shrug of his shoulders he replied, "Oh, I'm just gettin' a little concerned about our meat supply and some of the other stuff too. If the snow doesn't let up 'fore long, we might run low and maybe have to try to find some more meat. Course, that wouldn't be so bad, but tryin' to get through this snow could get pretty difficult."

"Difficult? Try impossible, even a horse couldn't

make it through this," declared Clancy as she motioned with her free arm towards the deep snow.

"Yeah, I been thinkin' 'bout that. I remember one bad winter with the folks and Pa made some snowshoes outta ash wood and rawhide. I think I might try to do somethin' like that."

"Well, I guess it's best to be prepared, I s'pose. But you might need to make more'n one set so you don't go out there by yourself. It might help to have somebody along to help carry the meat, ya' know."

"You're right, as usual," he begrudgingly admitted and continued, ". . . there's some Ash back behind the tack shed, it'll be tough getting' it, but I think I'll make a try at it. We've got some elkhide that'll make good rawhide and maybe enough for a couple sets. Yeah, I think that'll work," he mused as he began to picture the task before him.

The lay of the land was such that the cabin was about two miles distant from the mouth of the valley that opened to the great basin of the plains where the Cherokee Trail and the Oregon Trail crossed en route to the great West that drew the wagon trains full of settlers. The Platte river's headwaters were farther to the South but the river wound its way through the East side of the valley as it hugged the Medicine Bow mountains. Away from the protection of the mountains, the mouth of the valley gave way to the plains and less snow accumulation, but the opposite was true the farther upriver from the cabin. As the valley narrowed and other streams fed into the North Platte, the depth of the snow was greater. Usually elk herds, buffalo and deer gathered in the lower reaches of the valley because of the lesser snow, but this winter's accumulation was taking its toll on the winter range and the animals as well. Caleb knew he might have to travel a considerable distance to find game and he wasn't sure there would be game to be found.

Almost three weeks had passed while Caleb worked at fashioning the snow shoes. What with seasoning and forming the wood frames, cutting and stringing the rawhide and experimenting with formulating a protective coat with pine resin, bear grease and whatever else was handy and considered a possible solution. The final product passed inspection but it remained to be seen if the practical application measured up to expectations. There were few additional snowfalls and most amounted to nothing more than shallow dustings. The trees had surrendered their offerings to the sun and now stood with bare outstretched green pine boughs that contrasted with the snow covered terrain. An examination of the depth of the remaining snow compared to the porch railing revealed the overall depth had settled almost six inches but not enough to relieve the concern regarding ample meat supply. It would be at least a couple of months before the trails would be navigable by horseback or on foot, and Caleb was certain their current supply would be depleted before then. After cleaning off the table of all his scraps of wood and rawhide, he looked to Clancy and said, "I think I'll try these things out come mornin' and see if we can get some fresh meat."

"Who ya' gonna take with you?" asked Clancy.

"I'm thinkin' maybe Brewster, he seems to be capable

of handlin' a pretty good load so he'd make a passable pack horse, don'tcha think?"

She chuckled at her husband's comparison of the young man to a pack horse, but as she pictured the growing young man's shoulders and chest, she had to agree with her man. She nodded her head and said, "Probably, but you'll have to be careful with him. Although he's gettin' big as a mountain, he's still a youngster and doesn't make all the right choices, ya' know."

"Yeah, I know, but the only way he'll learn is the same way I did and that's by the doin' of it."

When Brewster was told at the supper table that he would be accompanying Caleb, his excitement seemed to boil over. "Gosh, ya' really mean it? That'd be great, I was about to go bonkers stayin' cooped up in that cabin yonder. I mean you fellas," motioning to the other men, "are fine and all that, but I was gettin' tired of starin' at them four walls and we've read all them books over an' over so many times I almost got 'em memorized."

The others looked at the broad shouldered young man that was bigger than all but Reuben and grinned,/ but also showed their envy at not being a part of the planned outing. Caleb picked up on the expressions of the others and added, "If this works, then the next trip a couple of you fellas will get to wade through the snow on them things," as he pointed at the snowshoes standing in the corner. Their expressions reflected their acceptance of the possibility of other excursions and they turned their attention back to devouring the meal before them.

Knowing they would need all available sunlight, the

two hunters departed the cabin at the first hint of dawn. This was the coldest time of the day when the cold of the night was driven deep into the coverings the men wore and before the heat of their exertions warmed the pair. They stayed near the tree line where the trees protected from drifts and trudged their way toward the mouth of the valley. The difficulty of breaking trail and having to walk with feet wider apart plus trying to find a rhythm of movement with the awkward contrivances made the travel slow and exhausting. Several rest stops were required but with few places of shelter or places to rest, the going was slower than expected. They alternated taking the lead and breaking trail giving the follower a bit of respite but they tried to maintain as steady a pace as possible. Finally about mid-day they found themselves clear of the tree line and overlooking the broader mouth of the valley. There were several areas that the wind had blown free of snow and revealed clumps of sage brush and patches of stiff brown buffalo grass. Farther in the distance they could barely make out what appeared to be larger clumps of brown and as they shaded their eyes from the almost blinding glare of the sun on the nearby snowdrifts, they recognized the quarry as a small herd of buffalo. The men looked at one another and grinned but were too tired to make any other acknowledgment. Finally Caleb said, "Let's move back by them trees yonder and have us some hot coffee and a bit to eat and then we'll figger out what we gotta do ta' get some fresh buffler steaks."

Their trek nearer the buffalo was watched by the burly beasts but with the poor eyesight of the big animals, the men were not perceived as a threat. Most of the woolies continued to graze, while others lay upon the sun warmed and wind cleared soil, with little attention paid to the figures now several hundred yards distant. The men made it a point of not approaching directly toward the beasts but angled the movements to appear they were bypassing the big animals. When they were about two hundred and fifty yards from their quarry, the men stopped and dropped their packs as Caleb instructed, "Brewster, you stand easy but keep your weapon ready and I'll take the first shot and if I don't drop one, then you can have at it." Caleb spoke from his position with one knee on the ground and the other uplifted for an elbow rest. But before he took aim, his motion was interrupted by a nudge from Brewster as he said, "Uh, Caleb, lookee yonder," motioning with his head to a slight knoll to their left. Standing back from the crest and out of sight of the buffalo but within view of the men was a cluster of Indians that were looking at the herd of buffalo. There were two horses held behind them, apparently for packing meat, but the men were too far away from the buffalo and there was little cover to shield a stalk. As Caleb watched, he noticed the movements of a couple of the Indians as they motioned to one another in the direction of Caleb and Brewster. "They've spotted us, now what?" asked Brewster. Caleb looked up at the standing young man and back to the Indians and said, "I think they're wantin' some meat too, but I'm thinkin' they can't get to 'em without a rifle an' looks like all they got is bows. Maybe we can help 'em a mite."

He resumed his shooting stance, but before taking

aim he handed four of his paper cartridges to Brewster and said, "Hold these ready for me." Then taking aim, cocking the hammer and setting his rear trigger, he slowly squeezed the front trigger. The resulting explosion was such that even the Indians jerked in surprise, but when he quickly reloaded and fired three additional times with each shot dropping a buffalo, the Indians chattered as the herd trotted some distance away. Caleb rose, reloaded his rifle and cradling the weapon in his left arm, walked toward the group of Indians with his right hand raised palm open and greeted the men with a simple "Ho" and began to communicate with sign language. They were surprised but with the white man showing no hostility they waited while he explained that three of the downed buffalo were for them and that he and his companion only wanted one, and they could even have the hide from his buffalo. They smiled and chattered and gestured among themselves and as a group, white men and Indians together began the task of skinning and dressing out the fresh kills.

THE BRIGHT SUN DID LITTLE TO DISPEL THE temperatures that hovered around the zero mark. As the men split the guts of the buffalo they dodged the rising steam and feverishly worked to finish the task. Difficult during good weather, the cold magnified the challenge and the warm flesh and blood did little to stay the cold from the men. By the time they deboned their choice cuts and strapped the large chunks of meat to their makeshift packs and were ready to start the return trek, the sun was low in the West and the shadows were lengthening. With a wave and a shout to the newly made friends, Caleb and Brewster retraced their steps to their cached snowshoes. It had been difficult before but now with the additional weight of well in excess of a hundred pounds of meat for each pack, the journey would be a considerable challenge. From the cabin to the kill site was close to five miles but the journey from their present location would be about half that distance. Caleb remembered the morning's jaunt had taken over three hours and now the return would require more than that. He looked to the West and realized the sun was resting on the treetops of the distant mountains and would soon disappear, leaving them with less than an hour of daylight. He shifted the weight on his shoulders and began the return.

With each lift of the heavy snowshoes he wanted to curse the contraptions but at the same time he was thankful for them. He knew any attempt at bucking snow this deep without the help of snowshoes would be an invitation to the death angel. At that thought he began to pray, *God, we sure could use some help here. You know we need this meat and I'm thankin' you for lettin' us get it, but now we gotta get it home and both of us are plumb tuckered out. Think you could see your way clear ta' givin' us a little more ambition or sumpin'?* And he struggled on putting one snowshoe foot in front of the other. The moon was showing its first quarter and provided little help, but the snow and the stars lit the way as they retraced their path. Suddenly Caleb thought he heard a growl from behind them. He stopped and twisted his body to look to their rear and spotted three black and grey wolves slowly trotting in the same path. With the smell of fresh blood and meat, the men were a temptation the pack couldn't resist. The shadowy pursuers were still some distance behind and Caleb told Brewster to go past him and continue on the trail, "I'll be right behind ya' but I can reload faster'n you and maybe I can change their mind. But let's try to put some distance behind us first." Brewster picked up the pace and now with the familiarity gained by the full day of practice, the men were able to speed up their shuffling gait. But the wolves refused to give up their pursuit. Yet the men continued to try to elude the pack. Suddenly from the side of the trail a black shadow launched itself at Brewster and he could only lift an arm at the last moment preventing the big wolf from sinking his bared teeth into his throat. The charge tumbled both man and beast into the deep snow and that was all that saved Brewster from the attack. The young man quickly drew his knife from the belted scabbard at his side, put there after the butchering of the buffalo and to hold his coat tight around him, and launched himself at the foundering wolf.

At the first attack by what was apparently the leader of the pack, the rest of the wolves ran to join in the fray. But Caleb had twisted around and with a shot from his rifle held at his hip the discharged slug caught the first wolf in the chest and threw him back against his followers. But they would not be so easily discouraged and vaulted over the carcass to resume their attack. Caleb struggled with his heavy coat in search of his tomahawk and snatched it free just in time to swing and hit the wolf, now mid-air in his launched attack, in the side of the head and splitting his skull just in front of the ear. The outburst of a squeal and a howl distracted the last wolf so that it hit the shoulder of Caleb and fell to the deep snow at the side of the trail. As the grey wolf whirled in the loose powder Caleb saw the fire in its eyes and the bared teeth of determination as it sought footage to once again launch itself at what he perceived as fresh meat. But the wolf was to be disappointed as the blade of Caleb's tomahawk buried itself between the fiery eyes. As the big wolf crumpled before him, Caleb searched the semi-darkness for Brewster and he saw the young man rise from the snow as he struggled to free his snowshoe bound feet from under the carcass of the big black wolf. Although the attacking canine had repeatedly tried to sink his teeth into the arms of the young man, the thick leather coat had protected him, but he had teeth marks to tell stories about.

Just shy of two hours saw the men making their way by the dim moonlight back up the trail to the cabins and the welcome sight of candle light on the porch. If the moonlight wasn't enough, the added glow from his wife's smile gave plenty of guidance through the deep snow for their return to safety and warmth. The other men were at the main cabin as well and Caleb was happy to relinquish the duty of storing the fresh meat to the waiting men. But before they put it all in their cache, they made certain to slice off enough steaks for the next night's supper.

"We heard a shot just after dark, was that you?" asked Clancy with concern showing in her voice.

"Yeah, just a little hindrance to our way we had to take care of, but nothin' to be too concerned about."

"And just what is it you're not telling me?" asked Clancy as she assumed her motherly stance of hands on hips. While Caleb and Brewster warmed themselves by the fire, the other men were busy storing the meat in the cache and Caleb looked at Brewster with a bit of a grin and started to answer but was interrupted by Clancy, "It wasn't Indians was it?" she asked with fear in her eyes.

"Nah, we already took care of them earlier today."

"Whaaat? You mean you ran into Indians?"

"Well, we didn't exactly run into 'em, more like spent a little time with 'em."

An exasperated Clancy stomped her foot and said, "Mister, you better start explainin'!"

With a chuckle from both Brewster and Caleb, they began a tag team explanation of their encounter with the Ute hunting party and the sharing of meat as a peace offering. "They were pretty happy with us too," explained Brewster as he rubbed his hands together and stared at the flames in the fireplace.

"And . . ." probed Clancy obviously referring to the last rifle shot she heard.

"Oh, you mean that last little fracas?"

"Fracas was it, and just what do you mean by a fracas?" she fumed as her temper was rising.

"Well, as I think about it, it was probably an answer to prayer," and at the confused look of his wife he continued with his explanation, "See, I asked the Lord to give us some ambition or sumpin' to get us home, and He did, but not the way I was hopin', see it was just a couple little ol' wolves that was hungrier'n they shoulda been. Thought they'd invite themselves to supper but we showed 'em, didn't we Brewster?" he explained as he looked to the young man to avoid the blistering stare of his wife.

She approached the two and gave them a cursory examination, noticed the marks on Brewster's arm and pointed, "And is that what you mean by 'showin' 'em'?"

"Ah that ain't nothin' Momma C, really it ain't. We just kinda rolled around in the snow a bit , that's all."

The entrance of the three men from the cold changed

the focus of the conversation as the men crowded around the fireplace to warm chilled hands and immediately detected something in the air with the three that now seated themselves at the table. Clancy was scowling at her husband as he tried to explain, "Well, it ain't like we invited them or nuthin'." She lifted her hands to the table and pulled the arm of Brewster closer for an examination in the candle light and said, "You better put some o' that salve I made up on those 'fore they get infected or something."

Caleb turned to the others and said, "In the mornin' a couple of you need to go back down the trail about a mile or so and pick up some pelts we left there. I'm sure they'll still be there but you might want to be sure an' take a good skinnin' knife with you." He knew Clancy was thinking they had encountered only two wolves and it wouldn't do to add to her frustration and worry to know there were four big wolves involved in the attack. But that could wait until tomorrow.

THE SOUNDS OF RUSHING WATER WERE ECHOING across the valley as cascades bounced off ice shrouded boulders and blocks of winter's remnants fought for passage way. The bright sun of the early spring was wreaking havoc on the previously unspoiled landscapes of white as the once fluffy flakes melted into tiny rivulets taking their winter companions with them as they retreated from the glaring sun. Clancy sat uncomfortably in the newly fashioned rocking chair wrought by her loving and attentive husband who sought only her comfort. The wretched time of morning sickness was past but her cumbersome form had yet to reach its limit yet the redhead struggled no less. But if anything could temper her discomfort it would be the blue skies and warm sun of this bright spring day. Caleb joined her on the covered porch as the bright rays of morning peeked under the overhang and warmed the couple. They were enjoying the quiet of the morning together having bid their goodbyes to the four hunters that were excited about getting out of that ". . . infernal cabin!" that had held them captive for the last several weeks.

Chance and Colton teamed up to hunt the black timber behind the cabins while Reuben and Brewster chose to go farther upstream and work the valleys and isolated meadows of the higher reaches of the mountains on both sides of the river. With the addition of the two horses donated by the attackers Bear and Catman, there were plenty of packhorses for the optimistic hunters to pack out any meat and hides of animals taken. While the brothers were hunting together they took one pack horse but Reuben and Brewster anticipated splitting up and hunting opposite sides of the river so they each led a pack mule in anticipation of a good hunt. It was mid-morning when Reuben reined up and collaborated on the plan for the day. "So Brewster, which side you wanna take. This hyar one," he said motioning with his head to the East side of the river and the black timber that started a short distance away, "or over yonder? Caleb says them mountains yonder are the Sierra Madre, which means Mother mountains, don't know why they call 'em that cuz they ain't no bigger'n any others we seen." Reuben let his gaze wander the rugged mountains and the black timber that was interspersed with granite outcroppings and escarpments. The range of mountains had many ravines and gullies that carried runoff from the white caps that still clung to the topmost peaks of the range.

Brewster looked from one side of the river to the other and thinking if he went to the East side, he would have to cross the river but if he stayed on this side, he could just cross the valley and would soon be into the timber. Looking at Reuben he said, "I think I'll just let you tangle with the river and I'll take to the timber over yonder," motioning with his head to the West.

"All right then, you just pay 'tention to whatever you choose to do, cuz when yore by yoself ain't nobody gonna be thar to pull yore fat outta the fire," warned Reuben thinking about the tendency of the young man to show more than his share of impetuous behavior. But the big stevedore knew Brewster needed to be trusted and given the opportunity to prove himself and he believed the young man that had grown to the size of a much more mature man would do well. With a wave to one another, the two friends put their heels to their mounts and set to their tasks of providing meat for the family.

Reuben continued upstream searching for a more propitious crossing to make his way into the beckoning black timber. Within a short while a snow melt fed stream coursed its way from the timber and intercepted the Platte. Upstream of the fork a flat meadow provided a shallow crossing that had already surrendered the ice flow to the fast flowing stream. The doney and gravel strewn river bottom showed through the slightly muddied water and made an easy crossing for Reuben and the pack mule. Spotting a game trail that led at an angle across the sloping hillside, he set to and began his vigilant watch for recent sign of game. He knew this was the time when bear would come forth from their winter's hibernation but it was also the time the timberline bucks would come to the lower climes for fresh sprouts of spring flowers donkey and grasses. Elk that had migrated to the flats for the winter would also be making their way to the mountain meadows and thicker timber as the cows sought out a protected place to give birth to the expected calves. Soon the bulls would be leaving the herds and searching out the companionship of other bulls and the young bulls that had recently been expelled from the herds would be searching out the new territory that might someday become their exclusive domain. He also knew the timber would not harbor any buffalo as the big woolies would be herding up and searching for graze in the flats. But everyone was anxious for fresh meat and wouldn't be too picky about what was brought home.

Considerably downstream from Reuben but still in the foothills of the Medicine Bow range, the Threet brothers were beginning a stalk of recently spotted elk anticipating an early success to their hunt. The small herd was gathered in a clearing that showed some grasses that remained from the previous summer and with heavy bowed heads from struggling under the snow, the grass promised nutrition to the hungry herd. "The breeze is to our face, so you move thataway through the timber and when you get set, take your shot and I'll be ready to take mine," instructed Chance to his younger brother. Colton nodded and backed away from the stone promontory and began his workaround through the timber. Now mid-day with the sun high overhead, the warmth came on his shoulders as he stealthily worked through the trees. The few spots of sunlight revealed the strapping frame of the tow headed man as his long strides covered the distance swiftly. A tall ponderosa beckoned the hunter and he leaned against the big trunk as he lined his sights on a brown collared bull. He slowly cocked the hammer, timing the click of the hammer with the creak of a nearby snag of timber that slowly swayed in the breeze and rubbed against another. Setting the rear trigger he moved his finger to the smaller forward trigger, sighted the brass blade between the buckhorn sight at the rear, he drew a slight breath, let it out and squeezed off his shot. The explosion was echoed from his brother's Hawken and as the smoke cleared, the meadow showed empty save two carcasses of the majestic elk now offered as meat for the hunters.

Colton stepped from behind the towering pine and waved at his brother as he rose from his crouch upon the boulder. Simultaneously they said to one another, "Good shootin' brother!" and with wide grins met at the carcass of the larger bull taken by Colton. Having already shed their antlers, the two bulls were prime game and would provide considerable meat for the hungry men. Caleb had said they wanted a considerable supply smoked and put up before the herd of cattle and the drovers showed up come summer. They knew there was a lot of work before them and the gathering of meat was just one part of their preparations as they sought to establish a cattle ranch in this wilderness.

The brothers were the closest to home and the first to arrive back with the fresh meat. With plenty of daylight left, they set about fashioning drying racks and gathering wood for drying and smoking the meat. The best wood available would be the mountain ash and aspen neither of which would give off any pitch laden soot that would tend to give a poor flavor to the meat. But with snow still on the ground in the tree shaded areas, the only dry wood available was from the dead branches of these same trees and that forced the men to extend their search farther than preferred, but such was necessary and the wood was soon gathered. Caleb had gathered some willow and chokecherry branches with which to fashion the racks and he and Clancy had readied the racks while the brothers sought the wood. Now the smoking of meat would begin.

Reuben's hunt was proving to be nothing more than a good ride in the timber. The only fresh tracks he spotted belonged to an early riser of a black bear but fortunately he saw nothing more than tracks. Most bear were rather temperamental when they first exit their den after a long winter's nap and were neither good meat nor good companions. Reuben's continued search led him in a downstream direction across the ridges and gullies of the foothills of the Medicine Bow. The closest he came to any game was hearing what he thought to be a small herd of elk busting through the aspen grove near the crest of the hill but out of sight and reach of his rifle. He continued on his quest but as the long shadows of late afternoon warned him of the coming end of the day, he dropped from the timber, sought a river crossing and made his way back to the cabins. He was hailed by Caleb as he and Clancy finished the racks and Reuben made his way to the corrals to free his animals.

As he walked toward the couple now seated on the porch, Caleb said, "Where'd ya lose the boy?"

Reuben chuckled and said, "We split up 'fore noon. He wanted to try the timber down yonder in the Sierra Madre, I think he just didn't wanna cross the river. That boy never was very fond of them river crossin's, 'specially after he saw that feller go under on our way out here."

Caleb's memory of the event brought a pensive look to his face and he added, "Can't really blame him for that, I reckon," then looking up at Reuben he added, "but it looks like you crossed it a couple times and did O.K., but I didn't see any meat on that ol' mule did I?"

"Well, the onliest thing I saw was bear tracks, but bear track soup don't feed nobody, so I left 'em where they were."

Clancy giggled at his remark and dropped her hand to rub Rowdy behind his ears and said, "But if'n you had followed those tracks, you mighta made soup for the bear."

Reuben grinned at her suggestion and said, "Well, I think I'd pass on that, sides this ol' darky's too tough for anybody's soup."

The brothers returned from their wood gathering and had to rub it in to Reuben how they were successful with their hunt and he was skunked to which Reuben replied, "I guess I'm just an old softy, cuz when that thar bear begged me not to take him cuz he didn't wanna be eaten by you two, I just had to give in and let him go back and finish his nap."

The laughter of the extended family was interrupted by the sudden clatter of hooves and the appearance of the pack mule and Brewster's horse with his saddle slung under his belly. The animals trotted over to the corral rail and looked back over their shoulders at the startled group as if asking to be let in to their corral. Both animals appeared to be frightened and seemed to shiver as they stood by the rail. The men ran to the animals and settled them down with gentle strokes and soft words, "Easy boy, easy now, you're all right, but where's Brewster?" spoke Caleb as if the animals could answer. The men gave both animals a thorough inspection as they removed the saddle and gear, searching for any sign of trauma or anything that would tell about Brewster. There were no claw marks and no blood and nothing that told of the happening and the whereabouts of Brewster.

THE TRAIL INTO THE THICKER TIMBER BECKONED
the young hunter and he reined his horse to the well
shaded cut between the tall fir and spruce trees. The trail
was littered with the castoff needles and branches from
the previous summer that were matted down with the
moisture from the winter's weight of snow. The black
mare shuffled along the trail with her head slowly
swinging side to side in time with her gait. Brewster
scanned the trees for any sign of movement or stationary
fur that would indicate the presence of game. Occasionally glancing at the twisting trail before him, he noted the
crest of a slight hill and the trail that followed just below
the skyline. As the path once again entered the timber,
Brewster thought he caught a glimpse of movement and
reined in his horse. Standing in his stirrups he sought a
view over the slight crest but was unsuccessful. He
pulled his Hawken from the scabbard, ground tied his
mount and crept to the crest to find the source of movement. Slowly lifting his head above the clump of scrub

oak that now obscured his view; he saw five Indians moving horseback and single file along another game trail across the intervening ravine. He immediately dropped below the brush and craw-fished back to his mount. Leaning against his saddle, he pondered what he should do, for if he continued on this trail, it might intersect the one across the way and he would be confronted by the Indians. He decided to cut through the timber to a lower trail that he thought would lead him through the trees and into a park he noted earlier.

Brewster stepped into the stirrup and swung aboard the black mare reining her into the timber to search a way through the maze and onto the lower trail. Within about one hundred yards, the trees opened to reveal the sought for trail. With the previous trek causing him to have to lean back to the rump of his horse due to the steep incline, now on the crossing trail he stopped for a short rest for him and the animals. While they sat still, Brewster surveyed the hillside and the openings through the timber for any indication of game. He noticed the steep slope from the trail to the brush filled ravine below and listening closely he could make out the sound of a small stream of runoff that cut through the brush.

A slight nudge of his knees and the black started a slow walk on the trail. Suddenly the horse stopped with uplifted head and ears pricked forward. Thinking it was the Indians, Brewster reached down his left hand to the horse's neck and spoke softly to encourage the mare. "Easy girl, I know, I know, we'll just wait here but be ready," he spoke as his eyes searched the trail. The mare swung her head down to the bottom of the ravine and back to the trail before her and her nervousness was readily apparent to her rider as she began to tremble beneath him. He knew the presence of Indians or man would not cause this kind of alarm and Brewster searched high and low for whatever was scaring his mount that now began to prance side to side as if searching for an escape. The slight bend in the trail obscured the forward view where the horse's eyes were riveted but suddenly the source of fear made itself known as a huge Grizzly lifted erect on his hind legs and blocked the trail. This was a sight that was seen in just an instant as Brewster was forced to grab for the saddle horn with his free hand and refusing to release his grip on his Hawken. The rearing horse screamed out a whinny as it whirled to make an escape. This sudden movement unseated her rider and with her rear hooves slipping on the downhill edge of the trail, Brewster was catapulted over the precipice and down the steep slope toward the thick brush below. As he tumbled, he lost his grip on the rifle and the second somersault brought the crown of his head upon a large boulder and the last thing Brewster saw was a cloud of black descending and obscuring the dust and branches that grabbed at his buckskins.

The five Ute of the small hunting party stopped instantly when the leader raised his hand. They all had heard the scream and whinny of the horse that followed the ground shaking roar of the Grizzly. These hunters were well aware of the power and danger of an enraged Grizzly and knew the wisdom of being certain of the location of any nearby threat. Their leader, Lame Deer, listened closely and suddenly Sings to the Moon, who was at the back of the group let out a short bird call and pointed to the crest of the opposite hill. They watched as a big momma Grizzly led two brand new cubs as they scampered over the crest and dropped into the thick timber behind the group. Spotted Owl, directly behind the leader, said "Maybe we should go see what happened to the horses, my brother," as she nodded with her head in the direction of the opposite hillside. Spotted Owl was just one year younger than her brother but had proven herself not just a good hunter but a warrior as well. Their father was the leader of this band of Ute and he expected both his children to prove themselves as his and worthy to be leaders. The Ute were not quick to accept a woman as a warrior but were willing to accept Spotted Owl for she had bested nearly all the men of her age at all the games of skill and cunning. But on this hunt, her brother had taken his rightful place as leader and now wisely listened to his sister. "Yes, we will go to see what has happened with the horses. They might be a prize to be taken."

Their horses were a bit skittish as the smell of bear was still strong but the firm hands of their riders kept them to the trail. As the small party rounded the slight bend in the trail, the sign was evident that this was the location of the confrontation. Crooked Leg had dismounted to examine the tracks and told Lame Deer, "This was the horse, a white man's horse, and the other was the long eared pack animal. They fled down the trail." He continued to look at the sign and saw where the horse stumbled at the edge of the trail and looking over the edge he saw the sign of the rider's fall. Pointing in the direction of the fall, Crooked Leg said, "I think the white man is down there." The rest of the party quickly dismounted and moved to the side of the tracker and looked to the brush below, "Yes, I see him there, in the brush," said Horse Killer as he pointed below.

"Go and see," instructed Lame Deer to Horse Killer and Crooked Leg. The fifth member of the party, Sings to the Moon, stood on the trail holding the leads of the horses and moved to the edge of the trail craning for a view of the bottom of the ravine. He watched as his companions slid and scrambled their way down the steep hillside. As they carefully approached the twisted form that was partially obscured in the brush, they saw he had a broken leg and several places of torn skin where the disheveled buckskins revealed flesh. When they neared the still form, they watched for signs of life and a slight movement of his ribs indicated he lived. Reaching through the entanglement, they grasped his arms and lifted him free. The man was unconscious but breathing, barely. His head was scraped and bleeding, a sizable gash at his hairline caused a trickle of blood to race down his cheek, a tear at the left shoulder showed another gash that was seeping blood. "He is badly hurt, but he lives," shouted Horse Killer to those on the trail.

With the aid of braided rawhide ropes and the help of those on the trail, the two rescuers soon brought Brewster to the top of the slope and laid him down on the side of the trail. Spotted Owl quickly assessed his wounds and with evident experience quickly ministered the necessary aid. She had dispatched Horse Killer to get four sapling branches to fashion a splint for his leg and within a short while had the patient ready for travel. Spotted Owl was the duplicate image of her brother with the same sturdy frame and height. Taller than most of the other women of the village, her stature and confidence intimidated any potential suitors but didn't concern the woman. She was strong but not muscular and there was no mistaking the fact she was a woman but not one to be argued with so when she told the others to lift the injured man to her horse so she could hold him erect for their return journey, they simply obeyed her direction.

On the trail for less than two hours, the hunting party stopped at the uplifted hand of the leader and war chief, Lame Deer. Before them and making their way through scattered spruce trees were three elk. The hunters dropped from their mounts without any direction from their leader and scattered into the trees. These men were well experienced at taking the monarch of the woods and knew stealth was demanded for them to get within bow range. Spotted Owl remained still and held the unconscious white man against her, he had shown no sign of wakefulness and she now sought to keep him silent. Within moments, the whispers of arrows were followed by the solid thud of impact and the grunt of the brown caped elk as two of the three stumbled to their knees while the third vaulted to the side and disappeared into the nearby thick aspen grove. The four hunters, to ensure the kill, doubled their chances with two arrows into each animal and were now jubilantly approaching the carcasses before them. Spotted Owl led their horses as she directed her mount with knee pressure to the edge of the clearing. She summoned Crooked Leg to assist her in lowering her burden to the ground while they waited for the butchering of the elk. Their return would be a joyful one and would probably result in a village wide feast, even with the unexpected visitor.

THE VILLAGE OF THE YAMPARIKA UTE PEOPLE WAS well situated in a wide park on a broad shoulder of the low ranging Sierra Madre Mountains. Surrounded by towering fir, spruce and pine with run-off streams on the North and South edges, it was a beautiful setting for the scattered wickiups of the people. This was their semi-permanent camp where they repeatedly returned after extensive hunts for the migrating buffalo. Each of the brush huts were unique with some having a similar shape to the hide teepees used when they moved and others dome-like, but each was situated with the doorway facing the rising sun. With frames of bent and bound saplings and coverings of bark and branches from Aspen and pine, these lodges were somewhat unique to the Ute people. Whenever the village went on the move, they would use the hide covered teepees favored by the plains tribes, but when they were in their more secure and familiar home grounds, the wickiup was the favored dwelling of the people.

As Brewster began to stir to wakefulness, the sights and sounds around him were startling. As he came full awake, he tossed side to side with his eyes searching for anything familiar but the furnishings and trappings that surrounded him were foreign to him. When the blanket covering the entrance to the lodge was flipped aside and the shadowy image of a woman entered, Brewster tried to sit up but dizziness overwhelmed him and he dropped back to the blankets as he grabbed at his head.

"Ahh . . .you are awake. Good. I was beginning to wonder if you would sleep all day," said the woman as she let a glimmer of a smile cross her face. Brewster lifted himself to his elbows and looked at the woman that knelt at his side. She was somewhat attractive with long braids that fell down her shoulders and were braided with bits of fur and ribbon. Her buckskin tunic had quillwork across the shoulders and a row of tiny trade bells across the chest. Fringe hung from the shoulders and down the sleeves. Brewster thought she was at least as old as Momma C and maybe a little older. He looked at her and raised one hand to his head and winced at the lump and soreness. Then looking at his leg he asked, "Is it broken?"

"Yes, but it is not bad. You will heal O.K. but it will be some time."

"Where am I? Is this your house?" asked the nervous young man.

"Yes, this is my lodge and you are in our village. We are the Yamparika Ute people. I was with a hunting party when we found you. Your horses were spooked by a Grizzly and we found you in the ravine among the bushes."

"You were with the hunting party? I didn't know women went on the hunting parties?"

"I am a warrior and my father is the leader of our people. His name is Walkara and I am Spotted Owl."

"What will happen to me," asked Brewster with concern in his voice. He had heard many tales about captives of Indians and how they were tortured and killed but this woman didn't seem to be afraid of him or ready to torture and kill him. She seemed to be genuinely concerned about his condition.

Spotted Owl smiled at his obvious fear and explained, "One of our war leaders told us you were one of the men that killed the buffalo for us and helped us. So it is only right that we do the same for you."

With the reassurance from Spotted Owl and his remembrance of the time he and Caleb had killed the buffalo on the winter hunt, Brewster relaxed and leaned back on his elbows with a grin of relief as he watched Spotted Owl change the dressings on his injuries. She was putting some kind of ointment on the wounds and packing some type of compress which was held on by strips of cloth. "What is that stuff you're putting on me there," asked the curious patient.

She looked up at the questioning young man and said, "This is made from bear root," motioning to the ointment, "and this is moss. These have been used by our people for many generations. They will help you to heal quickly."

"Bear root? Ain't never heard of it."

"Some white men call it osha. It is good for many things. Some even use it to keep rattlesnakes away."

"Ya don't say, well I'm all for that. Ain't never been friendly with any kind o' snake my ownself."

"All things the Great Spirit or the Creator makes are good and we should be thankful for them all," admonished Spotted Owl as if she were teaching a child.

"How long ya' think it'll be 'fore I can walk on this leg?"

"With help, you can walk now, but do not put your weight on it. If you need to go to the trees, I can help you."

"Help me? I can't go to the trees with you," he stated exasperatedly showing his embarrassment about even mentioning such a thing in front of a woman.

Spotted Owl laughed at the young man and explained, "I will help you and I will leave you to be alone and I will come back for you."

"Oh, oh, O.K. then, well I need to go to the trees as you said."

Brewster was surprised at the woman's strength. She was not as tall as his almost six feet, but she was taller than most women he'd been around and stronger too. With his arm over her shoulders and her arm around his waist and holding to his hand upon her shoulder she easily helped him to hop along on just one foot until they entered the trees well away from the lodges of the village. Leaving her patient in the care of a cluster of aspen, Spotted Owl turned away and started back toward the edge of the clearing as she told him to call for her when he was ready. Just a few moments were required for him to complete his business before he called for his nurse. As she walked with her head down and her hand to her mouth he could tell she was snickering and he was certain his embarrassment was entertaining to the woman. As she arrived to help him he asked, "Don't you have a man of your own?"

Her expression sobered and she replied, "I have not found a man suitable to share my lodge with and I do not find it necessary to do so."

The manner she displayed upon answering his question brokered no room for explanation and Brewster wisely chose to keep his silence on the subject. Upon returning to the wickiup, she assisted him as he was seated on the blankets and she began preparing food for her hungry patient. Silence hung like a wet blanket after a storm and Brewster knew he had violated some code of privacy that she held close. He asked, "I don't understand why you are helping me. It seems to me that with you bein' a chief's daughter an' all, that they'd have somebody else doin' it."

"I found you, so I have chosen to tend to you. Do not take what I am doing as anything special for it is the way of our people. You will stay here until you can travel and then you will leave."

As she spoke it was without emotion and made Brewster once again feel as if she was simply teaching a child, but there was nothing he could do to change that and he decided he would do best by just minding his manners and doing his best not to rile anyone, especially his caretaker. He had no doubt she was capable of anything since she was a respected warrior of the people.

His short walk to the trees had given him a brief look at the village and the many people that were part of this band of the Ute. Even if he was physically able, he doubted he would be able to escape with the many people around them. He had noted the number of warriors that had watched as he and Spotted Owl made their short walk and knew that he would probably be watched at all times. He reminded himself again to just mind his manners and not do anything that would give anyone an excuse to finish what the fall down the hillside had started.

"So, you said when I get better I can leave. Does that mean I'm not a prisoner?"

Again she grinned at her charge and clarified, "No, you are my guest. I will get you a walking stick that will help you get around and you will be free to move about as you wish."

She handed him a bowl of stew and a wooden spoon as his stomach growled in anticipation. He caught a whiff of the steamy concoction and readily started spooning the stew to his mouth. He downed the delicious stew and asked for more which the woman readily provided. She was pleased at his reaction to the food and willingly continued refilling his bowl until he slowed down after the fourth bowl. Brewster was well known for his appetite and eagerly devoured his new favorite food.

"What was that? That was delicious," declared the young man as he leaned back with his hand on his stomach and a broad smile painted across his face.

"It is not polite to ask, but I will tell you. The meat was fresh elk heart and the rest was potatoes, onions and amaranth."

"Well, it was very good. You're a good cook, probably

as good as Momma C," declared Brewster enthusiastically.

"Momma C? Your mother is with you?"

"Nah, Momma C and Caleb kinda took me in back in
St. Louie an' I came out West with 'em as part of the
Buffalo Brigade. But we parted company with the
brigade last fall back at Fort Laramie. We got us a cabin
o'er on the Medicine Bow not too far from the Hot
Springs. Ya know where they are don'tcha?"

"Yes, we know where your cabin is and where the
Springs are, we go there sometimes."

"You know where our cabin is?" asked Brewster
surprised.

"We knew when you came to the valley and when
you made the cabin."

The young man was speechless as he thought about
the many ways they had tried to keep their presence in
the valley hidden, but he remembered Caleb saying the
Indians probably knew everything from the first day they
arrived. *Guess he was right all along, but now what? Are
they gonna run us out or let us be?* thought the young man
as he watched his caretaker tending to the lodge and
her guest.

It had been a troublesome night with everyone wanting to start searching for their missing member, Brewster. When the horse and pack mule returned without the young man there was no end to the speculation as to his whereabouts and condition. Knowing the area of his hunt would take him in closer proximity to Ute country most thought he had been taken by the Indians. But hope held a tenuous grip on their hearts when they saw no sign of blood or battle on the returning animals. Well before dawn, Caleb was busy packing his gear while Clancy readied breakfast for the searchers. Reuben and the brothers were saddling the horses and readying the pack mule by the feeble light of a lantern that hung from the harness peg on the corner post of the shed. Working in silence, the thoughts of the men were only on Brewster and what they might find. Their extended family had been fortunate since the first day they came together as they departed Fort Laramie last summer. With the wilderness fraught with constant danger from Indians, animals and the many challenges of the unknown, the extended family had suffered no loss and little injury. Now their thoughts were on the possible loss of the youngest member of the group and the consequences of such a tragedy.

"How long do you think you'll be gone?" asked Clancy as her concern for Brewster mixed with her fear for her husband and the boys.

"Well, I'm thinkin' I'll just take Colton, leave Chance here, and if we don't find the boy as soon as I'm hopin' we'll send Colton back with news and letcha know what we'll be doin'," replied Caleb as he continued with packing the last pannier of the pack. They were preparing for no more than a week but with enough provisions for several days. He knew this search could encompass a considerable amount of country and time and it was always best to be prepared for anything. He too had thoughts of concern and fear that chased one another through his mind but he tried to focus on the task before him so they could leave as soon as possible.

"I don't need no babysittin', it might be better for you to take 'em all," said Clancy knowing her husband would refuse to leave her alone, especially with her pregnancy in full bloom. She thought she would have a couple more months before the baby would make its appearance but trying to do the necessary chores around the place was getting to be quite a challenge with her condition such as it was.

"They ain't gonna be babysittin' ya' and you know that. There's plenty of work for them to be doin' and things that you don't need to be doin'," he firmly stated with a scowl on his face.

"Well, when we were with the Arapaho, their women didn't slow down just cuz they was with child," commented Clancy.

"And they didn't sleep in a cabin and have a feather mattress on their bed, either. But it don't matter no how, if you have to look at it as the boys stayin' fer my peace of mind and not yours, fine. They'll be stayin' anyway. 'Sides, we'll probably find the boy sittin' long side the trail just waitin' fer a ride and we'll all get home by dark."

"Yeah, if you thought that, you wouldn't be packin' 'nuff food fer a week," said Clancy as she looked over her shoulder at her man. She continued her tending with the meat and gravy and added, "Breakfast's 'bout ready. Ya' wanna call the fellas?"

Caleb usually spent the first light of day in prayer at his prayer log on the edge of the clearing, but first light was yet to make its appearance and the preparations for the search took all his attention. Now as the entire group assembled at the table, he began his prayer, "Our Lord and Our God, we are thankful we can come to You today and You know we stand in dire need of Your help. We don't know what we'll be facing on this search, but we are asking that you take care of the boy and keep him safe till we get there. We also ask for help in our search and that you keep everyone safe both at home and on the trip. Thank you for our food and strength for the day. In Jesus name we pray, Amen."

It was an unusually silent group that seated themselves at the table, but the silence was soon dispelled with the usual sounds of hungry men devouring a breakfast of meat, biscuits and gravy before they started on an uncertain trek. Chance was disappointed he would not accompany the rest of the men but he understood the need for someone to remain behind. "Do you want me to start cuttin' some o' them Lodgepole pine fer them corrals you were talkin' 'bout?" asked the tow headed young man as he looked toward Caleb hopeful of an answer that would give him something to keep him busy while they searched.

"Yeah, I think that'd be good. We're gonna need quite a few of 'em cuz we'll need to build a couple of pretty large corrals accordin' to what our partner, ol' James Heffernan said. I think one of 'em'll be for the horses or remuda he called it and the other'n be for separating the cattle. So, we'll need a sizable bunch of poles, but when ya' cut 'em, make sure you leave some. We don't wanna jus have a big bare spot in the middle of them skinny trees, they need to grow back some."

The rest of the breakfast eaters looked at Caleb with confused looks on their faces and Colton asked, "Bare spot? You mean like all the other 'bare spots' that are all throughout the mountains, you know, parks and clearin's an' such?" It was a common sight to see the clear parks and open meadows amidst the thick black timber where the Creator had provide both shelter and graze for the many animals of the mountains. The thought that Caleb was thinking another bare spot would be unacceptable was confusing to the listeners.

"Ahhh, you know what I mean. Not just a bare spot, but little stumps all over and branches and such."

"Oh, you mean like the stumps and branches and deadfall we see everywhere else?" asked Clancy getting into the mood of poking fun at her husband.

"All right, all right, just do whatever you think's best!" instructed a frustrated Caleb with a grin of surrender.

Reuben led the way as they returned to the place where he and Brewster had parted company the day before. Pointing to the vague trail through the scrubby brown grass left from last summer's growth he said, "He headed out yonder. I went a bit farther upstream and went back into the timber back East there, and he said he was headin' up into the black timber to find a park, you know, one of them bare spots," he chuckled as he looked at Caleb, "to see if he could find some meat."

Looking in the direction of Reuben's point, Caleb stood in his stirrups and surveyed the distant tree line looking for any indication of a trail. Finally dropping to his seat he said, "Let's follow that bit of a trail through the grass just in case that was from him and that lazy footed pack mule. As we near the tree line we'll spread out and see if we can find a game trail or some indication of where he went." Again, Reuben led the way as the small caravan of searchers moved across the grassy plain. The brown grass had been laid low by the winter snow and the new green shoots were struggling to break through the rich black soil below. Occasionally a sprout of a blue lupine or small daisy teased the grassy meadow with just a hint of color, but for the most part, spring was still struggling to make its entrance. The easy gait of the horses shuffled through the grass and carried their burdens toward the trees. As they neared the tall timber, an evident break in the cluster of skinny fir trees told of a game trail that cut behind the trees on an angle across the face of the mountain. All the men had spotted the opening and comment was unnecessary as Reuben continued on the trail. As soon as they were in the timber, Reuben stopped and dismounted to look at the trail before him. Caleb went to his side and the two men examined the tracks on the aspen leaf and pine needle strewn path. Dropping to one knee and reaching down to trace the outline of the tracks, Caleb looked up at Reuben and said, "There's two sets of tracks here, one goin' and one comin' but there don't seem to be any others. And from the looks of 'em, the horse was carryin' weight up and empty comin' down. So whatever happened, it's on up the trail."

The two men stood side by side and looked up the trail as it wound through the trees before them. They remounted and started on the track again and within less than a quarter hour, they spotted where the animals had stopped and Brewster had dismounted. Once again, Caleb stepped down to examine the sign and looking at the footprints of Brewster where he left the trail, Caleb made hand signs to indicate he was going to follow and for the rest to wait. Handing the reins of his Appaloosa to Reuben and slipping his rifle from the scabbard, he started up the hillside to follow the footprints of Brewster. As he approached the crest, he saw where Brewster's knee made an impression and he dropped to his knee to examine, then slowly rose to look over the crest of the hill and survey the ravine and opposite hillside. He easily spotted the trail that cut through the trees across the facing hillside and could see the evidence of tracks, even from this distance, the freshly turned soil showed black against the nearby pine needles. He scanned the area around where he stood, spotted Brewster's tracks going back down the hillside and Caleb followed. Back at the horses, he moved up the trail just a short ways and saw where Brewster had taken off downhill through the trees. He trotted back to the horses and explained to the men what he had discovered. He swung into his saddle but kept his rifle in hand as he took the lead and reined his horse to follow the evident sign of Brewster and his animals as they moved down the hill.

The slope was steep and the men had to lean far back on their mounts to maintain some semblance of balance as they let the animals have their heads to pick their way through the thick timber. Within moments they were out of the trees and on the trail that Brewster had sought and found. Looking back to see if Reuben and Colton and the pack animal were all on the trail, Caleb motioned for them to have rifles ready and to follow him. They kneed their horses to a walk and moved forward along the trail but it was just a short distance before they spotted the evident sign of a mishap. Scouring the trees for any sign of danger, Caleb dismounted and began to examine the sign of the startled animals and the scrambling on the narrow trail that led to the animals retreat. Reuben and Colton joined him as they looked at the hoof prints on the high side of the trail where the horse had spun after rearing and unseating his rider. "Looks like they were spooked by a Grizzly," said Caleb. Colton pointed to the tracks and disturbed dirt and rocks on the edge of the trail and as he walked to the edge of the steep hillside, he pointed and said, "Looks like Brewster got bucked off and went end over end down the hill."

Caleb and Reuben stepped to his side and shaded their eyes to see the signs of the fall, but Caleb pointed to his left and said, "But somebody else went down there and came back up, probably with Brewster. Those are moccasin prints and there's more up here on the trail," he said as he pointed the men in the direction of the uphill side of the trail. He walked to where he saw the sign and kneeling down said, "And here it looks like they laid him down," then touching a small stone with his finger, "there's blood here. He was hurt, but it looks like somebody tended to him and they put him on one of their horses." He walked a few more steps, examining the trail and lifted up his eyes to Reuben said, "I think there were five of 'em and they took Brewster with 'em."

Turning to Colton, Caleb said, "I want you to go on back to the cabin and tell Chance and Clancy what we found here. Tell Clancy me'n Reuben's gonna follow their trail and see if we can get Brewster back. It's a good sign that they brought him up and took him with 'em, cuz if they wanted to do him in, they'd just done it where he lay. So, I think we'll have a good chance at gettin' him back."

"You really want me to tell Momma C that Indians took Brewster?" asked Colton thinking he didn't want to upset her.

"She can handle it, both of us was practically raised by Indians so you won't be able to keep it from her. She'd figger it out anyway. Now go on, you can make it back before dark and she'll have a good supper for ya'."

Colton handed the lead for the pack horse to Reuben and mounted up and headed back down the trail not anxious to tell Momma C the news about Brewster. *Boy, I hope he's alright, it just wouldn't do for anythin' to happen to him, he's one of the family,* thought Colton as he reined his horse along the twisting trail and made his way to the grassy meadow. He knew Momma C was strong, but she was always the mother hen especially with the youngest of the bunch and he didn't know how she would take the news of Brewster being in the hands of the Ute Indians.

Brewster sat just outside the doorway of the wickiup leaning against a woven willow backrest. Watching the activity of the people he also noticed he was being watched. A young girl of about six summers had walked past him and shyly looked his way as she passed and now on her return she looked a bit more boldly his way. She stopped and turned to look directly at this strange visitor to her village and he watched as she examined him with her eyes. Her gaze lingered on his splint and the split leg britches that revealed a swollen and bruised leg. Using a long twig she carried she reached toward the leg and looked at him with a question and he responded with, "It's broken, I broke it when I fell off my horse." Realizing she could not understand him, he thought for a moment, then motioned for her twig which she surrendered to him. He began drawing pictures in the dirt beside him to explain with stick figures what happened and she watched with occasional giggles breaking through her otherwise stoic expression.

She squatted down beside him to see his drawings more closely and pointed at the stick figure and then at him and asked with her eyes and a pointed finger if that was him. When he nodded his head she smiled and laughed as she pointed to the horse and then his leg and made it clear she thought it was funny that he got bucked off and broke his leg. Chuckling at her response, he nodded his head and said, "Yeah, I guess it is funny." Then he added with a crude drawing and upraised arms accented with a growl and a snarl, about the bear. The little girl was frightened and ran away with a quick glance over her shoulder to make sure he was not following her. When he raised his arm and said, "Wait, wait, I didn't mean to scare you!" a voice came from behind him that said, "You didn't scare her. She was doing what her mother told her to do if she ever saw a bear and you made her think you were a bear, although a pretty skinny one," said Spotted Owl with a bit of a snicker. "She will probably come back to see you just to be sure you didn't turn into a bear. Sometimes mothers warn their children against danger by telling them the danger could be a bear in a different costume."

"Well, that ain't fair, cuz I sure ain't no bear," pouted Brewster.

"But you don't understand. A bear is not always a bad thing. One of our most important ceremonies is the Bear dance when we welcome the new Spring and life begins anew. You see those people coming with the travois behind the horse?" she asked as she pointed to a family group that was coming into the camp. "They are part of the Mouache band of the Ute people. They and many others will be coming to our camp in the next few days as we prepare for the Bear dance. It is a time for celebration and a time for families to come together and for young people to find sweethearts."

Brewster looked up at Spotted Owl as she worked to prepare a pot of stew at the cooking fire outside the wickiup. She looked back at him and smiled, "So, you need to watch yourself, because some young woman might come for you and since you can't run away, she might just get you."

"Whatchu mean, get me? You don't mean they can just come and get whoever they want? Surely not?" he begged as he looked at his host with concern etched across his face.

Giggling, she responded, "Oh, you don't have to worry, you're too pale and too skinny. The only ones that would want you are the ones too ugly or too fat to get anyone else. But since you can't run away". . . she left him hanging on her statement as she turned back to the pot to hide her broad grin and to keep from laughing out loud.

"Maybe I better stay inside then cause if they can't see me they can't get me," grumbled Brewster. But he was stopped when Spotted Owl said, "I won't feed you if you're in there. You must eat out here with me." He rolled his eyes and his head as he searched the village for any sign of some woman looking at him with designs on her mind. He was relieved to see no one looking his direction and when he heard Spotted Owl try to stifle her laugh he realized she had been kidding him. At least he hoped she had been kidding. Changing the subject, Brewster asked, "You know Spotted Owl, you said I was your guest and all, but if I know Caleb, he's gonna come lookin' for me. What'll happen if some of your people catch up with him lookin' for me, they won't kill him will they?"

"If he comes in peace and does not try to fight with our people, he will not be harmed. Is this Caleb the other man that helped our people when you killed the buffalo?"

"Yeah, he is, matter o'fact, he's the one what did all the shootin' and it was his idea to give the buffalo to your people. He could see all they had was bows and arrows and the buffalo were a bit too skittish for any kind of stalk, so with his big Sharp's he just pulled up and shot 'em. He's all fired good with that big gun of his," he commented shaking his head as he remembered the hunt. "Course, he might have some o' the others with him when he comes and I sure wouldn't want any of 'em gittin' scalped or nuthin'," he looked at Owl and shook his head, "Ya think we oughta tell somebody or sumpin'?"

"My people know about your people and they already know someone will probably come. Who are the others?" she asked as she tended the stew and looked over her shoulder at Brewster.

"Well, there's Caleb, he's kinda like the leader an all what with him and Clancy bein' kinda like Ma and Pa to the rest of us. Then there's Reuben, he's a giant of a man that's blacker'n a shadow at midnight but he's a good man. An' the other two are the Threet brothers, Colton and Chance. They ain't twins but they could be they look so much alike what with their yeller hair an' all."

"And the woman, Clancy you called her? Is she the same as the one you called Momma C?"

"Yeah, she's like an ol' mother hen, takin' care of us an' all. She's quite a woman, her and Caleb were raised by Indians up in the Wind River mountains," stated the young man. Spotted Owl turned to look at her patient with a frown on her face as she asked, "They were raised by people in the Wind River Mountains?"

"Yeah, both Caleb and Clancy are whatcha call orphans, they lost their real folks when they was young and they was taken in by Jeremiah and his woman among the Arapaho."

Spotted Owl looked at Brewster and he could tell something was going on in her mind and whatever it was had unsettled her somewhat. Finally she asked, "Does this Caleb think of himself as an Arapaho?"

"Why no, he's a white man, just like me. His folks was white and his adopted Pa is white, nah, he's just purty smart when it comes to Indian stuff. You know, like bein' able to talk their lingo and doin' the hand talkin' and stuff."

Spotted Owl seemed to relax a mite and returned to her work at the fire. Little did Brewster know that the Arapaho and the Ute had long been enemies. Although in Spotted Owl's lifetime there had not been any conflicts with the people to the far North. Most of their battles had been with the southern ranging Cheyenne and some of the far roaming Comanche from the South. She would be careful and watch if the man from Brewster's camp, this Caleb, came to her camp and her people. She thought again of the people of Brewster and asked,

"So, this Clancy is the only woman with all these men? Is that the way with your people that one woman has so many men?"

The surprised look on Brewster's face brought truth to his comment as he laughed and said, "Oh no, you got it all wrong. Clancy is Caleb's woman, as you say it, but she's more like a mother to the rest of us. And a real good mom she is too!" His emphatic statement gave another smile to Spotted Owl as she asked, "So, will some of these others come with Caleb when he comes for you?"

"Probably, but if you're thinkin' 'bout them girls again, I don't know."

"The big black man, does he have a woman?" said Owl trying to sound as disinterested as possible.

Brewster laughed and said, "No, he doesn't, but it'd sure take a lotta woman to handle that man. He's almost as big as that Grizzly that scared my horse, an' I'm sure he's probably stronger too!" With her back to her guest, Spotted Owl let a conniving smile spread across her face. She turned with a bowl of stew and offered it to Brewster and his mind quickly dismissed their entire conversation as he focused on the feast before him.

Holding her own bowl and wooden spoon, Spotted Owl tucked her legs beneath her as she leaned against the side of the wickiup. Brewster was intent on his meal and conversation was not on his mind, but the mind of Spotted Owl was busy with imaginations and wonder. She had proven herself the equal and even superior of every warrior in her village and her size and agility had added to the intimidation felt by the men. When they sought a mate, they looked for the small or petite sized woman that would cater to their every need and never threaten them in matters concerning hunting and battle. There had been a few that had expressed interest, partly because of her standing in the band with her father as their chief, but the interest soon waned when she refused to surrender herself to their will and way and forego her warrior status. The status of a warrior and proven hunter had been earned by her and her brother as a necessary part of their standing as the children of the chief and she would not turn against her father to please a man. But she was a woman and a woman that wanted a family but to find a man that would be her equal or better was a difficult task. She wanted a man she would be able to look up to as a man, a warrior and her physical mate. That meant her choices were few, for she was a big woman and a hard to please woman. The thought of this man that Brewster described set her to thinking *I wonder if he is the mate the Creator has for me? The way this young man described him, he sounds like he could be, I wonder?* She smiled as she let her mind form a picture of this giant of a man and what he might be like. Then shaking her head, she returned to her practical side and dismissed the thoughts of a silly girl to return to her responsibilities and tend to her patient. His dressings needed to be changed and she would have to wrap his leg with the splint and she knew he would complain. *White men, why do they always complain?*

ONLY A MOMENT WAS SPENT WATCHING THE retreating form of Colton as he started his return to the cabin bearing the news of the captured Brewster. The sun was quickly advancing across the cloud littered blue and the shadows were starting their Eastward advance as Caleb and Reuben started on the trail in pursuit of the missing member of their wilderness family. The tracks of the mounts of the Ute had left deep impressions in the damp soil of the shade darkened path. With this being the trail the hunting party had followed to the site of their confrontation with Brewster and the same trail for their return, the tracks left a well churned trail of black moist dirt. As Caleb looked at the path before him he realized their quarry was not concerned about leaving an easy to follow trail. This could mean they could easily overcome anyone in pursuit or if they were followed to their camp, they would not fear discovery. That confidence could only come if they were aware of the possible pursuit by Caleb and company. Knowing they would not be able to mount a surreptitious raid for the rescue of their friend, they would be left with the only possibility being a direct and blatant confrontation by riding straight into their camp. Just the thought of willingly riding into a village with an overwhelming number of warriors brought second thoughts to Caleb. These thoughts and more were occupying the man as the day was drawing to a close and Reuben spoke from behind, "Uh, we gonna keep on goin' or are we gonna make camp for the night?"

"What? Oh, yeah, sorry I was too deep in thought. I didn't even notice how late it was getting. Yeah, we need to find a spot to camp, I don't think we'll make their village before dark and I don't think we want to go in there at night."

Reuben shook his head as he realized Caleb was not as aware of his surroundings as he usually was and Reuben was concerned. However, within moments Caleb reined his horse off the trail to a small clearing just back from the path and motioned for this to be the site of their camp for the night. It was just a short while until the two men had the gear removed and horses hobbled and a small fire started for some coffee. Reuben put a small frying pan on the edge of the fire to warm up some Johnny cakes and strips of smoked meat for their supper while Caleb tended to the coffee pot. Their fire was at the edge of the clearing and not much bigger than a bowler hat. Made from dry wood, what little smoke emanated was filtered through the outstretched branches of the long needled ponderosa behind them. Finishing off their supper and sitting back with the warm cups of coffee wafting its aroma before their faces, Caleb began to share.

"You probably noticed the tracks that huntin' party's been leavin' like they ain't too concerned 'bout anybody followin' 'em," said Caleb and looking at Reuben he watched the big man nodding his head. "I'm thinkin' they're expectin' us to be comin' after him. Ya reckon?"

"Yeah, believe so. And there's enough of 'em that they don't rightly seem to care if'n we catch up to 'em neither.
"

"I was thinkin' back to when that bunch of Utes visited the hot springs, remember? And when they were leavin' that one big buck raised his arm and waved like he knew we were there all the time."

"Yeah, I remember. So, you're thinkin' they been knowin' all 'long where we were and how many of us there are and that's why they ain't skeered of us?"

"Yeah, that's about it. I remember when I was livin' with the Arapaho. They always had scouts out and about and just about anything that was happening within miles of their camp, they knew what was goin' on and who was doin' what. Some tribes call those scouts Dog Soldiers, others have warrior societies that have that responsibility and I'm thinkin' these Ute know all about us."

"Maybe, maybe, but since they ain't come after us or attacked us, maybe they're tryin' to be friendly, you think?" asked Reuben.

"Yeah, I s'pose that's possible, or they could just be waitin' for us to come into their camp and then lift our hair."

Reuben lifted his eyes to Caleb showing the whites of

his eyes in the glow of the firelight and said, "Now that ain't very comfortin' to be thinkin' 'bout as we try to go to sleep."

"Well, if they know all about the cabin and everything else, they probably know about us followin' 'em so we might as well try to get some shut-eye. I'd like to get an early start in the mornin'," said Caleb as he crawled to his blankets.

The sun was just breaking through the treetops as the two searchers were well on their way following the trail of the hunting party. Caleb reined up and held up his hand to signal to Reuben to join him. The trail they were on was joined by another broader trail that also showed considerable sign of travel. "Lookee there, that's a pretty good bunch and they're pullin' travois. Looks like they're joinin' up with those we been followin' or at least goin' to the same place. Wonder what's goin' on?" With no answer coming from the big black stevedore, Caleb put the heels to his horses ribs and continued on the trail. Caleb led the spare horse they brought for Brewster while Reuben led the pack mule as their tracks mingled with the many travelers that had gone before them.

From the corner of his eye, Caleb saw movement and he let his hand drop to the butt of his rifle but made no other move. Slowly and casually turning his head, he noted a mounted warrior riding parallel to the trail about twenty yards distant through the scattered pines. He was watching Caleb and Reuben but made no move in their direction. Looking to his left he saw another warrior mirroring the movements of the first. Looking back over his shoulder to Reuben, he saw his friend nodding his head to indicate he had also spotted their company. Continuing along the trail, they were soon joined by two more warriors, one on either side, bringing the complement to four uninvited companions for their journey. Through the trees before him, Caleb could tell there was a clearing ahead and the smell of smoke warned him they were approaching the village. There was nothing they could do but continue.

The nearer they approached the village, the closer rode their outriders until as they broke from the trees, the warriors were by their side not more than three yards distant. Caleb reined up, dropped the reins to his horses neck and using sign language asked if there was an injured white man in their camp. One of the warriors rode up to the side of Caleb and spoke in English, "You look for your friend, the young man that was injured on the trail?"

"Yes. His name is Brewster and he is part of our band or family. Do you have him here?"

"What are you called?" asked the warrior without answering Caleb's question.

"I am called He Who Talks With the Wind but my white brothers call me Caleb."

"I am Lame Deer. Follow me," instructed the warrior.

Caleb and Reuben followed the warrior leading their additional animals and surveying the activity of the camp. They were watched but there was no alarm among the people for they continued their activity. It was evident there were preparations being made for something special. At the far edge of the camp a fence like barrier was being constructed with a large tree at the far end and an opening on the near side. Many cook fires blazed beneath suspended pots and skewered meats and several women were busily decorating tunics with beads and quills in fancy patterns. Caleb was reminded of the celebrations of the Arapaho people and knew this activity portended something special. He just hoped it wasn't some type of sacrificial ceremony to which he and his friends were to be special guests.

They were led through the camp and to the front of a trio of wickiups and were surprised to see Brewster seated outside the nearest one. He waved and hollered at them with a big "Hello! Boy am I glad to see you two!" He struggled to a more upright position but it was evident from the splint on his leg he was unable to rise. Caleb and Reuben dismounted and were surprised when a young man took the reins on their mounts and pack mule and motioned he would take care of their horses. Caleb didn't want to surrender his mount but the nearby warriors and their stoic expressions kept him from grabbing at his rifle as the boy led the animals away. Brewster saw his concern and reassured him with, "Ah, they'll be all right. He's just takin' 'em back of the lodge yonder. You'll be O.K."

As Caleb and Reuben started to approach their young friend, a woman suddenly stepped before them and said, "Are youCa-leb?"

Surprised Caleb responded, "Uh, yeah, and who might you be?"

Brewster interrupted with "Why that's Spotted Owl, she's the daughter of the chief and this is her lodge. She's the one that picked me up on the trail and been takin' care of me," then to Spotted Owl he said, "Spotted Owl, that's Caleb and that big feller there," motioning to Reuben, "is Reuben."

Ignoring Caleb, Spotted Owl looked up at the big man and smiled as she said, "Bear Chaser has told me about you."

"Bear Chaser?" choked Reuben as he looked at Brewster. "Bear Chaser?"

"Yes, we call him Bear Chaser because he chased a Grizzly bear from the trail before he was hurt," then smiling she added, "but it was just a small one with two little cubs." She looked back at Brewster and grinned at her patient. Looking again at Reuben she said, "You will join us for our meal?" as she motioned to the pot suspended over the fire. Reuben had already caught a whiff of the concoction from the pot and his stomach had growled its anticipation of food so Reuben said, "We'd be glad to Spotted Owl." But the food wasn't the only thing that had caught the big man's attention. The coy smile from the woman had the big man shuffling his feet in the dirt and dropping his head in embarrassment. But he didn't let his gaze wander far from this very attractive woman and she too let her eyes linger on his. She motioned for him to be seated by Brewster and she would serve them. Caleb stood dumbfounded and transfixed as he watched the two flirting with one another like a couple of teenagers. She had totally ignored Caleb and it was only by the motioning of Brewster that he took a seat on the opposite side of the injured young man.

Spotted Owl served Reuben a big bowl of the stew and handed him a spoon, then returned to the pot for another bowl and spoon which Caleb and Brewster thought would be for them. But she seated herself next to Reuben and began to eat the stew as she stared at Reuben. Brewster looked at Caleb and asked, "Uh, how 'bout you gettin' you and me a bowl of that there stew, looks like we ain't invited to their party." Caleb chuckled as he rose to retrieve their share of the stew for their meal. While Reuben and Spotted Owl spoke with one another to get better acquainted, Brewster began to fill in the details of his recent adventure. He told Caleb about the bear, "And it weren't no little'n either, that thing was standin' on its hind legs an was lookin' at me eyeball to eyeball and I was still on my horse!"

"Yeah, they do get pretty big, I know."

Brewster continued with his tale to include the background of Spotted Owl and her family, the history of the Ute and the Arapaho, "So, ya better be careful an' not git 'em riled up," he cautioned. When he told about the upcoming Bear Dance and the practice of the people to find a mate, he nodded toward Reuben and said, "I think she's lookin' at him as a possibility!"

Caleb glanced their way and saw that the two were pretty focused on one another and it sure looked like she might be thinking along those lines. He chuckled to himself and said quietly to Brewster, "Well, I think that'd be fine if they were to get together. They'd make a good couple and it wouldn't hurt to have a good friendship with the Ute. By the way, do you think you're gonna be able to sit a horse and come home?"

Spotted Owl happened to hear his question and she spoke up and said, "No, he cannot travel for some time.

We will keep him here until he can ride." Then looking back at Reuben she added, "But if you want to come and see him, you may come any time." Reuben looked at her and smiled. She stood and said to the big man, "Come with me and I will show you our village. You should meet my brother and my father." Reuben stood and she smiled broadly as she watched him stretch to his full height. She looked him over and unabashedly admired his physique and reached out to touch his large biceps and smiled.

THE RETURN TRIP TO THE CABINS WAS A PLEASANT one for the two friends as they reminisced about the recent happenings and the possibilities of the future. Reuben admitted being smitten with Spotted Owl and for the first time in his life he dared to dream about a future other than the solitary one he presumed was all he deserved. Caleb chuckled at the permanent smile that was borne by his friend, it was good to see the joy that brought the new expression to the big man. Heretofore he had been known as a sober and even somber man but those that knew him well knew him to be a thoughtful and friendly man that held friends and family close to his heart. But laughter and cheerfulness had been locked away amidst the trials and challenges of his previous life of slavery and hard work on the docks of St. Louis. On this short trip he was just as apt to be laughing and chuckling as not and it was surprising to hear him break out in song.

"Now Reuben, you've only known this woman a couple of days now so I don't understand the way you're actin'," kidded Caleb. "If I didn't know better, I'd think you were in love or sumpin'."

"Well, lawdy mercy Caleb, don't you think a black man can love a woman?"

"See, there ya go, talkin' 'bout love already. Next you're gonna be wantin' to build another cabin so you can bring her home with you."

"You really think I can? Build another cabin, I mean."

Caleb shook his head as he chuckled at the big man with the big heart and said, "Well, as fast as you're movin' we better get started on it first thing in the mornin'!"

As they reined their mounts up the slight hillside toward the cabin they saw Clancy standing with one hand on her hip and the other shading her eyes as she watched the two riding into the clearing with the empty spare horse and the pack mule trailing behind. Because they were laughing, she assumed they bore good news but she was bewildered at the absence of Brewster. When they were near she said, "All right, out with it, where's he at? What'd you do with him?"

As they dismounted Caleb responded, "Aw, them Indians like him better'n we do so we just let 'em keep him."

"You what? You didn't leave that boy with those Ute, did you?"

"Well, it seemed it was better'n leavin' him with the Grizzly he took a liken to."

"Caleb Thompsett, you better get up on this porch and explain yourself!"

He looked at Reuben as the big man laughed and said he would take care of the animals because they were friendlier than Clancy and he would have to do the explaining all by himself.

"Thanks a lot, some friend you are," declared Caleb as he turned to mount the steps to his waiting woman.

"Well, ya see it's like this, it seems Bear Chaser," but he was interrupted by Clancy as she said, "Bear Chaser?"

"Yeah, that's Spotted Owl's name for Brewster.'"

"And who's Spotted Owl?"

"Oh that's Reuben's new girlfriend."

"All right, stop right there, I've got to have a cup of coffee for this tale," exclaimed Clancy as she turned to go to the cabin. But her flight was interrupted by the clutch of her husband as he pulled her to him for a welcome home embrace and lingering kiss. As she leaned back to smile at him and take a deep breath she said, "You're enjoying this too much, the tale I mean. You just wait here and I'll get us some coffee for this windy tale of yours."

When she returned and took a seat in her rocking chair, he sat on the bench beside her and began to tell the story of the injured and wayward young man, the Grizzly and her cubs, the love sick couple and the planned cabin.

"A cabin? Already? Surely you're not serious?" queried a frustrated Clancy.

"It's not me that's serious. Wait till you see Reuben, then you'll see who's serious."

The mention of his name caught the attention of Reuben as he neared the cabin, having completed his duties with the animals. The big man was still smiling as he took the steps in one long stride and grinned at the couple on the porch. He appeared as all teeth and big eyes with dimples sinking deep in his dark cheeks as he said, "Evenin' Momma C."

Clancy looked up at Reuben and back at her husband and back at Reuben. Then turning again to Caleb she said, "I see what you mean."

Reuben just smiled and stepped off the porch with another long stride and followed the path to the men's cabin, humming all the way.

"If I hadn't seen it, I wouldn't have believed it. She must really be something."

Caleb began to tell her all about Spotted Owl being the daughter of a chief, a proven warrior and hunter and probably the most important woman in the village. "She's a pretty woman but she's bigger'n most, I think that's why she took a shine to Reuben right off. Course Brewster said he had told her about Reuben before we got there. Somethin' about a big celebration called the Bear Dance her people do this time of year and it's a time that the maidens go looking for a mate. He said she kept asking about him especially after Brewster told her he was a big 'un."

"What is it about you men anyway?" asked Clancy with a bit of a scowl on her face.

"What do you mean?"

"Well, like Ma and Pa, Jeremiah and Laughing Waters, she was a warrior and Shaman of her people. And her brother, Broken Shield, he married Pine Leaf and she was a war leader with the Crow, and now

Reuben and Spotted Owl, she's a warrior and leader of her people. Can't you men be happy with a woman that's just a plain ol' woman and not some warrior or something?"

"Nope, least not folks like my family. We want them special ones, you know, like you, you ol' Grizzly killer and warrior woman you," he said thinking back to their encounter with the Grizzly outside their cabin in the Wind River Mountains when she dropped the big bear with one well placed shot before he could kill her husband. Even before they were married, Clancy had often gone with the other women, Laughing Waters and Pine Leaf, on hunting trips and had repeatedly proven herself the equal of both women. She became proficient with bow and arrow, throwing both tomahawk and knife, and was an excellent marksman with her Hawken. She would never have to take second place to any man.

"Oh you, you know what I mean."

"Yeah, but it takes a lotta woman to tame a real man. And sweetheart, you done tamed me!"

The following morning, Reuben and Caleb joined the brothers in their efforts to down the timbers needed for the building of the corrals. The higher slope of the mountains yielded the close growing but slender lodge pole pine that were best suited for the corral fencing but they often grew on the steep slopes that were hard to access. The previous day's work of the brothers showed with a considerable pile of de-limbed poles that had been snaked out behind the mules. It was close and tiring work, but with the thick growth the men divided up the work and expedited the labor. Even though Caleb had both a one man and a two man saw to use in felling timber, these trees were more easily dropped with an axe. The base of these trees was about the diameter of the breadth of a man's hand and a sharp axe in the hands of Reuben would cut through the soft pine in three or four strikes. The brothers used tomahawks to top off the poles and remove any limbs that remained after the tree dropped to the ground. Caleb would drag two or three at a time behind a mule and would soon have a stack ready. Reuben had fashioned a skid to haul the logs behind the team of mules and by noon, the men were ready to haul logs to the site of the planned corrals and go on to the cabin for their noon meal. Clancy had promised a good feed for the hard workers.

Caleb and the brothers loaded a good stack of logs on the skid and secured them while Reuben hooked the mules into double harness and backed them up to the skid. The mules leaned into their harness and the skid easily moved across the damp soil to the cleared trail. Caleb and the brothers followed along behind and Caleb noticed Reuben visually measuring the bigger fir and spruce with an eye to a future cabin. He chuckled as he thought of the big man turned romantic and muttered a quiet prayer for God to give his direction and blessing. *Reuben deserves to be happy, Lord. I think it'd be good for both of 'em and you and I both know their meeting wasn't just an accident.*

As the men sat on the bench and the edge of the porch after their fine meal of elk steak, potatoes, onions, and Johnny cake, they basked in the warm sun that promised a green spring. Caleb was looking at the budding bitter root flowers that would soon show forth its pink blossoms on the low growing greenery. Farther down the hillside was a patch of the Indian paintbrush that would bring orange and red blossoms and soon the entire valley would be awash with colors of all shades and hues. The broad trail through the bottom of the valley was showing prickly pear cactus that would soon sprout yellow above the red apple like fruit at the end of the wide flat blades. As he let his gaze wander along the trail, he was surprised at some movement at the far end of the valley. He slowly stood to get a better look and the others noticed his movement and looked in the same direction to see the source of concern. As they watched, Caleb whispered, "Well I'll be doggoned, those are wagons."

"Where?" asked Colton as he stood to look.

"At the head of the valley, they must be followin' the Cherokee trail. I knew some wagon trains used it, but I just wasn't expectin' any," and looking at the rest of the men he continued, "this here trail connects to the Oregon trail and the Mormon trail. Folks comin' from down Denver way or South of there or maybe even Indian territory come thisaway to hook up to the Oregon."

They watched as the white bonneted wagons slowly snaked their way from the tree lined pass that came across what would later be called Cameron Pass at the far South end of the Medicine Bow Mountains. The white snake had crossed the North Platte farther upstream and now followed the trail to the West side of the river. All the wagons had a four-up hitch of horses and most appeared to be sizeable draft horses. The men on the porch were mesmerized by the unexpected sight and Colton spoke up with, "Looks like there's about twenty of 'em. That's a passel of pilgrims!"

"Sure is, and I'm hopin' they just keep right on a goin'," added Caleb.

CALEB'S HOPES WERE DASHED AS THE MEN WATCHED the white snake of a wagon train start to circle up within walking distance of the hot springs pool near the smooth flowing North Platte. Either the scout or the wagon master was familiar with the hot springs and planned on allowing the people of the train an opportunity to partake of the refreshing mineral waters. Caleb's shoulders drooped at the thought of so many people nearby with all the expected noise of neighbors and clutter of disrespectful travelers. He turned to Clancy and was surprised to see a cheerful smile on her face as she watched the activity in the bottom of the valley. "So, what are you so happy about, it's just a bunch of noisy greenhorn pilgrims that're gonna make a mess of things and be a bother while they're here. They can't leave soon enough for my likin'," grumbled Caleb as he scuffed his boots on the porch floor.

"Well, I was thinkin' it might be nice to pay 'em a visit. It's been quite a while since I've sat and visited with other womenfolk, and I think I'd like that," stated Clancy with her chin outthrust daring Caleb to countermand her determination.

His surprised look betrayed his selfish thoughts but he soon relaxed his expression into a glimmer of a smile as he responded, "You know, I guess I oughta be ashamed of myself. I wasn't even thinkin' 'bout that. Tell ya what I'll do, you get yourself ready and I'll saddle up the horses and we'll just go down yonder and introduce ourselves. That be O.K.?"

She smiled and leaned over to peck her husband on the lips and turned to the doorway and disappeared into the cabin evidently excited about the prospect of meeting new folks. While Caleb could easily be a hermit and never see another human being, except Clancy of course, for years at a time, Clancy was more the social type and enjoyed meeting and getting acquainted with people from all walks of life. Now the possibility of making new acquaintances put a new bounce in her step and a smile on her face. Though her movements were slightly hampered by her pregnancy, she easily readied herself for the anticipated visit and was soon seated on the porch awaiting her husband.

She had instructed Caleb to rig her horse in an Indian fashion with a cinched set of stirrups and blankets that would enable her to ride in a semi-bareback manner. Her protruding belly made it impossible for her to ride comfortably in her saddle. Caleb led the two horses to the stairs and led hers close enough for her to use the steps to make it easier to mount. After she was seated, Caleb mounted up and they reined their horses in the direction of the circle of wagons.

Several men were busy hobbling the many horses enabling them to graze on the remains of the grass from the previous summer and the few green shoots that were vainly trying to make their entrance into the sunlit meadow. Caleb and Clancy watched as several youngsters had been dispatched to the nearby trees for some firewood and the smaller youngsters were belly down at the edge of the running water seeing if they could spot a trout or maybe some minnows. Women were busy setting up their tables and preparing the fare for their evening meal and would start their cooking as soon as the firewood was available. It was a village on the move with an abundance of activity. Although not a large wagon train, it was sizable enough to leave a wide trail in their wake. With grass grazed down, trees and woods denuded of wood, roadway muddied and marred with deep ruts, and often cast aside items of furniture and other belongings that proved more burdensome than valuable. But for now, the presence of new faces and interesting people proved to be enticing enough to overlook the negative impact of the travelers.

As they neared the large group, Clancy noticed a couple of women that stood with hands on hips and shading their eyes as they watched the approaching visitors. When the two women recognized one of their visitors as a woman, they smiled and waved and motioned them to join their gathering. There was enough space between the wagons to ride their mounts into the circle and Caleb and Clancy were greeted with, "Howdy folks, welcome and come on and sit a spell," said one of the women. Clancy smiled and said, "Afternoon, and thank you. We thought we'd come down and visit with you all for a spell, if that's all right."

Caleb had quickly dismounted and now reached up to help Clancy dismount. The women had already noted her condition and looked at one another and smiled. When Clancy touched ground, one of the women pushed a ladder back chair in her direction and said, "Here ya go Missy, seat yourself."

"Thank you. My name is Clancy and this is my husband, Caleb. We live up yonder in the trees there," she said as she motioned in the direction of the cabin.

"You live here?" asked the women in unison with surprise in their voices. Then looking at one another, they laughed at their simultaneous answer. "Oh, excuse us, I'm Barbara Sparger and this is my friend, Barbara Brown. Most of the folks on the train refer to us as the two widow ladies," she snickered as her friend smiled. "So, you live here, and how long have you made your home in this place," asked the first Barbara as she motioned to the surrounding valley.

"Oh, we just built our cabin last fall, but we've been in the mountains for quite some time. Although just before we came back here we spent some time in St. Louis."

As the women continued their get acquainted conversation, Caleb walked away in the direction of a couple of men that appeared to be the ones in charge. They watched as the buckskin attired young man approached. The older man was sitting on a trunk next to the bed of the wagon and the younger man was leaning on the large rear wheel. The seated man was attired in a Lindsey Woolsey shirt over striped britches held up by wide suspenders and tucked into tall boots. He was a sizeable man with a full salt and pepper beard that did little to hide his red cheeks and red nose, but his eyes flashed a friendliness and mischievousness which gave him an immediate likable quality. A floppy felt hat was on his knee as he ran his free hand through his thinning hair. He watched Caleb as he approached and didn't move from his comfortable seat.

"Afternoon," stated Caleb, "looks like you folks have been travelin' a spell, gonna take a dip in the hot springs?"

"Some of 'em might. Familiar with it are you?" asked the big man.

"Yup, since it's in my front yard, you could say that."

"Front yard?" asked the younger man. He was also outfitted in buckskins but was clean shaven save for a handle bar mustache that drooped to the sides of his mouth. He was dark complexioned with coal black hair and dark eyes that had a bit of mystery to them. There was nothing alarming about the man but he had an air of quiet confidence that spoke of danger. He continued, "How can it be your front yard, ain't nobody lives around here?"

"We do, right up there in those trees," pointed Caleb. "We're startin' a cattle ranch and we're settlin' this area."

"But what about the trail?" asked the older man.

"Oh, by the way, I'm Caleb Thompsett, and as far as the Cherokee trail, it'll still be open. We don't mind travelers, after all, we've all been travelers at one time or another."

The relaxed stance of both men was evident at the answer from Caleb and the older man said, "I'm Jedediah McAllister, I'm the wagonmaster, and this here's Lucas Donavan, he's our scout. Would you care for a cup of coffee?"

"Don't mind if I do," replied Caleb as McAllister waved at a nearby cookfire and motioned for the cook to bring some coffee to the men. Caleb watched the grizzled older man with whiskers going in every direction bring three enameled cups of steaming brew to the confab and turned to the two men and asked, "Are you headed for the Oregon Trail?"

"Yup, most of these pilgrims have their hearts set on that country that so many folks have been talkin' 'bout that's s'posed to be heaven on earth. They're thinkin' they can build a house, stand on the front porch and throw seeds out and wait till the fall and harvest a great big ol' crop easy as you please. But other'n bein' a little deluded with their dreams, they're a purty good bunch o' folks. Say, you know much about the country 'tween here an' thar?"

"A bit, whatcha wanna know?"

"What about Injuns, hear tell of any problems?"

"Well, round hereabouts are some Ute, but they're not too bad. After they signed the treaty in '49 they been doin' a better job of mindin' it than most white folks. Course as you go farther, you'll be cuttin' across Cheyenne and Arapaho country. The Cheyenne are kinda unpredictable, but you can usually get along with 'em, usually. Then there's the Arapaho. Dependin' on the band you run up against, they can either kill ya' or befriend ya' so ya' gotta watch your step. Keep your folks close in, don't kill anythin' ya' ain't gonna eat, and don't shoot first."

"You seem to know a lot about them, why's that?" asked Lucas.

"Grew up with 'em," replied Caleb without explanation.

Clancy was pleased to learn that Barbara Sparger's husband had been a doctor and she had worked with him in his practice. "I was kind of his nurse but also a midwife," she explained. "I did most of the attending to the birthing for the womenfolk. They were just more comfortable with a woman, you know how it is," and continued, "Is this your first child?"

Clancy explained to the women about the loss of their first baby and her concerns about this one. "I've never let on to my husband about it, but I guess it's only natural after losing our first one."

"Do you have anybody that'll be with you for the birth?" asked Mrs. Sparger.

"Well, my Ma and Pa might be here, but I don't know, and they don't know for sure when the baby's due. We sent word to them before the snow and we hope they know, but we'll just have to wait and see."

"Well, my husband was a pastor and there were times when I held the hands of women as they gave birth, but other'n that, I wouldn't be any help, but Barbara there, she's birthed a lot of babies," said Mrs. Brown. "But, I'm afraid we'll be a long ways down the trail when the big event happens."

"Would you like me to examine you, maybe see if I can give you a better idea when the baby'll come?" asked Mrs. Sparger.

"Would you? Just knowing would help. I'm thinkin' I've got maybe a month left, but the baby's been pretty busy, kickin' an' all, so I really don't know."

When Caleb returned to the side of his bride, she smiled up at him and said, "The ladies have invited us to join them for supper, isn't that nice?"

"Uh yeah, it is. I guess the fellas'll figger out they've gotta scratch together their own supper. It'll make 'em appreciate you even more," stated Caleb as he smiled down at Clancy.

THE STILLNESS OF THE EARLY MORNING HARMONIZED
with the whisper of the early breeze through the pines.
The Eastern horizon showed as a silhouette against the
soft grey of the promise of a new day. Reuben's familiarity with the path between the cabins made his morning
walk one of memory than exploration. His mind was on
his day's destination as he rounded the trail at the corner
of the main cabin and continued on his way to the corral
that held the horses. All the animals were standing
hipshot with drooping heads but the Appaloosa stud of
Caleb lifted his curious eyes to the shadowy figure
approaching. A soft greeting from a familiar voice reassured the animal as Reuben grabbed a halter from the top
rail and entered the gate in search of his big bay for the
day's journey. By the time he finished gearing up his
mount and tying it off to the top rail outside the corral,
the sun painted the low hanging clouds with broad
strokes of orange tinged with muted reds. It promised to
be a fine day for a ride to the Sierra Madre and the camp

of the Ute to check on the state of Brewster and maybe get better acquainted with his caretaker, Spotted Owl. The thought of the Indian woman tugged a smile from the face of the big black stevedore as he turned to see Caleb standing on the porch with a steaming cup of coffee in his hand. With a nod of his head, Reuben walked to greet his friend and beg a cup of coffee for his start on the morning.

Caleb could tell by the guilty expression of his friend exactly what he had planned but he couldn't resist the opportunity to poke a little fun. "Well, it sure is a fine thing to know you're so concerned about the welfare of poor ol' Brewster. I didn't think you cared that much for the squirt."

Letting a subtle chuckle escape Reuben replied, "What with them Injuns keepin' him and we don't know that much about 'em, I figgered they need to know we was keepin' an eye on 'em, an all. You know, just to keep 'em honest and make sure he's gettin' the proper care and feedin'."

"Ummmhummm, I unnerstand. It's always best to make sure his nurse is doin' things the proper way too, don'tcha think?"

"You know, I believe you're right 'bout that."

Clancy heard the talk and now stepped into the doorway with another cup of coffee for Reuben and said, "Good Mornin' Reuben, goin' to check on our boy are you?"

"Well now how'd you know 'bout that, Momma C,"

"Maybe a little bird told me, you know, a little love bird," she snickered.

If a black man could blush, Reuben would have been as red as the Ute Indians he was going to visit. The three went back into the cabin to partake of a bit of breakfast to start the day and send Reuben on his way. Before they finished the brothers had joined them at the table and the family shared bits of chit chat regarding the plans for the day. They expected the wagon train to pull out and knew there would be ample work regarding the continuing construction of the corrals. There was still a considerable number of poles to snake out of the timber and skid to the site of the corrals as well as beginning the construction of the corral fences.

"While you two fellas go back to the timber to bring out them poles, I'm gonna start markin' out the boundaries of the corrals and mebbe start on some o' them post holes. I don't cotton to usin' that shovel, but it's gotta be done. So, don't take all day with them poles." Turning to Reuben he added, "I know your trip's gonna take the better part of three maybe four days, but we can sure use your help if'n you can make it back as soon as you can. If the boy ain't ready, maybe you can make another trip in a week or two to fetch him home. I'm sure Spotted Owl won't mind seein' you again," he grinned. The brothers stifled a laugh as they looked at an embarrassed Reuben then Chance added, "Yeah, an' maybe that'll give you time to build your new cabin. We," motioning to his brother, "were figgerin' on callin' it Reuben's Roost!" The cabin was filled with laughter as everyone joined in the fun and the embarrassment of Reuben was replaced with the comfort of knowing his friends only sought the best for him.

Reuben waved over his shoulder to the rest of the family as they scattered to their chores for the day. The brothers to the corral for the mules to skid the poles, Caleb to the tack shed for his gear to lay out the corrals, and Clancy returned to the cabin to continue her work on the blankets and bedding for the bassinet and the soon to arrive baby. As she turned she noticed the activity at the wagon train as they prepared to move out on their long journey of dreams. Remembering her short visit with the widow ladies, the two Barbaras, she wistfully thought it would be nice if they could stay until the baby came, just to have someone to visit with if nothing else. Little did she know that the two widow ladies had turned their wagon away from the train and were now heading up the hill in the direction of the cabin. A short while later Clancy heard the rattle of trace chains and the creak of wheels as the wagon pulled into the clearing. Clancy went to the door with a touch of alarm on her face but when she saw the women she broke into a broad smile and asked, "Ladies, what are you doing?"

They both laughed and Barbara Sparger said, "Well, we got to thinking about you and this here trip and we decided we could sleep in our wagon just as easy while it's settin' here as on the trail somewhere. And the wagon-master McAllister said there'd probably be another train through here before long if we decided to join up and leave then. So, if you'll have us, we'll just keep you company for a while."

"Have you, of course and tis' welcome you'll be," said the redhead lapsing into her Irish brogue with a tinge of laughter that showed her joy and relief. She was thrilled that there would be a woman with the experience of the midwife Sparger to be at her side for the coming birth. Although she still hoped Laughing Waters, the adopted mother of both her and Caleb, would arrive in time, just knowing there would be a woman of experience at her side was comforting. "Come in for a cup of coffee and a wee bit of visitin'," she added.

The women looked around and saw a flat spot near the edge of the trees, pulled the wagon onto the grassy area, dropped down and began unhitching the team. They had proven themselves quite capable of handling both the wagon and the team during the past three weeks of the trip with the wagon train and that experience showed as they quickly set their camp and tended the animals. As they stepped up onto the porch, Clancy exited the cabin with two fresh steaming cups of coffee and the ladies seated themselves as all three ladies were smiling so broadly it was almost too difficult to talk. Almost, but not impossible and the conversation began to flow.

Reuben made good time on the trail to the Ute encampment and arrived just as the pines in the West cradled the sun beneath the expanse of color that stretched the width of the sky and painted the horizon with the brilliance of orange in all its hues. The many cook-fires twinkled like earth-borne stars as they decorated the darkening village but Reuben well knew the way to the wickiup where Brewster was lodged. He knew he had been watched and followed for at least the last half mile before he arrived at the camp and the distant watchers now dropped off to seek their own homes and families. Brewster stood to greet his visitor but Reuben noted he still used his walking stick to steady his stance. Looking about he sought the familiar figure of Spotted Owl and was disappointed at her absence. As he reined his horse to a stop at the wickiup he was greeted by Brewster, "Hey there Reuben, boy it's good to see you. Come ta' get me didja?"

"Well, I came to check on you boy. How ya' doin'? They treatin' you O.K.?"

From behind him came the familiar voice of Spotted Owl, "Did you expect different?"

Turning to look at the woman, he couldn't help smiling as he responded, "Well, not really. I figgered you'd take real good care of the boy, and I see you have."

"Will you join us for our meal?" asked Owl as she walked past Reuben to the cook fire.

Brewster chuckled and quietly said to Reuben, "I think she's been expectin' you to come back just 'bout ever night. She'd walk around a bit lookin' yonder at the trail and now's the first time she smiled since you left."

His comment brought a smile to the face of the big man as he seated himself beside Brewster. Spotted Owl quickly brought the two men bowls of the stew that had been simmering over the fire and as she handed the spoons to the men she said, "It is good to see you," as she looked at Reuben. There was little conversation for the remainder of the meal but considerable looking at one another on the part of Reuben and Owl. Brewster was beginning to feel as if he wasn't even there and when he said he was going to turn in for the night, neither Reuben nor Owl acted as if they heard him.

As darkness settled over the village, Reuben and Owl were seen still sitting by the fire and talking with one another totally oblivious to the rest of the world. Such was the way of two people experiencing the pangs of love, it is the beginning of understanding and acquaintanceship that are the building blocks of a lasting relationship. But as the realization of the passing of time came upon them, Reuben said, "I'm gonna roll out my blankets back there in the trees and stake my horse nearby. But I'll be back here bright and early in the morning and I'm hopin' you'll be here waitin' for me."

"I will be here," she stated simply as she ducked her head slightly and looked up at Reuben under veiled eyelids.

The light from the dwindling fire reflected in her eyes and Reuben reached to her chin and with his massive paw gently lifted her chin and slowly came close to kiss her. Her eyes were open wide as she held still and experienced her first real kiss. As he pulled away, she smiled demurely, which was a movement totally out of character for a proven warrior and leader of the people, but one which further endeared her to the big man.

After a breakfast of fire grilled slices of deer steak and a leaf wrapped type of bread that was new to Reuben, the two started on a walk around the edge of the camp. The trail they followed took them on a circuitous route in and out of the nearby trees. When he asked about the activity of the people that appeared to be leaving, she told him about the ceremony of the Bear dance and how it welcomed the spring and was a new start for the people. "Many young people find mates and begin their new lives together too," she said as she intentionally looked away from Reuben. "At the conclusion of the dance, they leave prayer offerings at the tree," she pointed at the large tree at the end of the big enclosure that was the site of the ceremony, "and ask the Great Spirit for blessings for the coming year."

Suddenly bursting from the nearby trees a massive figure of a man came charging directly at Reuben shouting and screaming as he held a hide shield on his left arm and an upraised war club with his right. Clad in leggings, breechcloth, a bone breastplate and other accouterments, the big man was enraged and growled like a cougar attacking its prey. Reuben pushed Owl aside with his left arm and dropped into a crouch to face the attacker. He pulled his big Bowie knife from its sheath at his waist and raised it to block the coming blow from the war club. Although the man was big, Reuben in a crouch was still face to face with the attacker and he met growl with growl which startled his attacker but not enough to stop the charge. Bringing the club down in an attempt to crush Reuben's skull, the man was surprised when the uplifted knife was held unflinching and split the handle of the war club causing the bulbous head to flip end over end past Reuben's head. The big black man dropped his shoulder to meet the hide covered shield and bracing his feet became more of an obstacle than the attacker expected and with the sudden force from Reuben, the man fell backwards with a solid thud that bounced his head off the hardened ground. With arms outstretched, he lifted his head to look at his quarry and pushed himself up as Reuben backed away still in his crouch with his knife moving back and forth and with his lips pulled back in a snarl he said, "I don't know what your problem is boy, but you done bit off more'n you can chew."

The Indian rose slowly and warily to his feet and looked from Reuben to Owl who now stood about five feet to the side of the combatants with an angry look on her face. The attacker bit out the words, "You have my woman!"

"Bear Paw, I am not your woman! I told you I would never be your woman!"

"You heard her, she's not your woman. She's my woman!" declared Reuben. Owl looked at him and let a smile begin to paint itself across her face. She relaxed her stance and crossed her arms at her chest and said, "I am his woman!" and motioned with her chin toward Reuben.

Bear Paw let out a roar that rattled the needles on the nearby pines and drew the attention of several nearby men that came near to see the conflict. As Bear Paw charged, Reuben noticed the man had drawn his knife and now held it low behind his shield. As he came near, Reuben feinted to the right and when Bear Paw stepped that way, Reuben quickly went to the left and back handed the big Indian with the haft of his knife against his temple knocking the man to his knees. Reuben quickly stepped behind him, slipped his hands under his arms and lifted the man off his feet with a roar that mimicked that of an enraged Grizzly. As he lifted, he reached his hands behind the man's head and bent his head forward. Still holding his knife in his hand, he said, "Now Bear Paw, I can cut your head off or I can break your neck or you can call it quits and admit that Spotted Owl is my woman. Now, what's it gonna be?"

The big Indian squirmed and twisted and kicked trying to free himself. Before this he had always been able to use his brawn to overcome any opponent and had never been lifted off the ground like this, much less held here and threatened. But Reuben wasn't sure Bear Paw understood him so he said to Owl, "Tell him what I said, I don't wanna kill him if I don't have to!"

In the Ute dialect she quickly and angrily told Bear Paw his choices and as the Indian relaxed his squirming Reuben heard him say, "You are his woman."

Looking at Owl for confirmation he was pleased to see her smile and nod her head so he released the big man. As he dropped to his feet, Bear Paw was muttering as he bent to pick up his knife. Reuben picked up the shield and handed it to the man and with his right hand outstretched for a handshake as a sign of friendship. Bear Paw looked up at Reuben with a surprised expression, down at his hand, over to Owl and with Owl's nod and motion, Bear Paw shook Reuben's hand and laughed with Reuben at the start of a good friendship.

LAME DEER AND HIS FATHER, WALKARA, STEPPED from the crowd that gathered at the ruckus between Bear Paw and Reuben. The two men looked from Spotted Owl to Reuben and back again for they heard what the rest of the crowd heard of the exchange between the combatants and Spotted Owl. Although most of the village had gossiped about the budding romance between the big black man and their favored daughter, nothing had been spoken openly between Spotted Owl and her father, Walkara. Owl's mother had gone to her eternal rest almost eight summers before when the village had repelled an attack from marauding Cheyenne that sought to steal horses and women. Cloud Walker, Owl's mother, had also been a proven warrior and had fought valiantly by her husband's side but an errant arrow had downed her and she crossed over before the battle was done. Spotted Owl was a young girl and watched the entire battle from within the family's wickiup and saw her mother die just outside the door as she defended her home. Walkara had chosen another woman to warm his robes but when Spotted Owl had proven herself as a warrior she established her own wickiup and chose to live alone, until now.

As the two men approached, Spotted Owl showed the due respect and she dropped her eyes to the ground until her father spoke. "Is this true, my daughter, what I heard?"

"What did you hear my father?" asked Owl as she lifted her head to her father showing a proud lift and a slightly protruding chin.

"That you have chosen this man as your mate?" he asked as he motioned to Reuben.

"We have chosen each other, father. He has proven himself worthy just now as he defeated Bear Paw and chose not to kill our brother warrior."

Walkara looked at the big black man and said to him, "Big Bear, have you chosen this woman as your mate?"

"Uh, yeah, I have, I want her to be my wife. I want to take her to my home," stated Reuben as he stepped to the side of Spotted Owl and put his arm around her. He had not missed the chief's reference to him as Big Bear and knew that when a chief gives a man a name it is because he is respected as a man and a warrior. Reuben appeared to swell his chest a bit as he stood beside his choice.

"Then you will come to my lodge so we can smoke the pipe together," stated the chief more as a command than an invitation as he turned his back and walked away.

Reuben looked down at Spotted Owl and met her

eyes as she turned to look up at her choice with a broad smile. She turned to face him and put both arms at his waist and pulled him close as she said, "Will you touch my lips with yours again?"

Without answering but simply bending down he gently pressed his lips to her as he pulled her tightly to him and let the kiss linger as he was filled with an emotion that brought wonder to his mind and joy to his heart. As they pulled apart, he saw she still had her head upturned and her eyes closed as if she expected the kiss to continue so he chose not to disappoint her.

When they parted to breathe again, she said, "It is an honor to smoke the pipe with the leader of our people. He will also want to know more about you."

"Ain'tchu comin' too?" asked Reuben with a touch of concern in his voice. The idea of meeting alone with the chief gave him certain reservations about what he should and should not do for the last thing he wanted to do was to inadvertently offend her father.

"No, even though I am a warrior of the people, I am a woman and the daughter of my father who is talking to my future mate and I cannot be there," and she smiled somewhat mischievously and continued, "it will be O.K., if you do or say something wrong, my brother will kill you is all." She giggled at his reaction and shoved him on the arm as they started on the way to the chief's lodge. He knew she was kidding but it didn't relieve his concern.

The three men sat cross legged around a small fire that was more for light than warmth. The blanket at the doorway was held back as it was bunched on a peg and did nothing more than cast the faces of Walkara and Lame Deer in shadows. Reuben realized that was the purpose, for the light was directly on his face and benefited the two men as they watched his expressions to their inquiries. When Walkara lit the pipe, he offered it to the four directions, the heaven and the earth, pulled a smoke from it and then handed it to his son on his right. Lame Deer repeated the movements and then handed the pipe to Reuben. Reuben carefully mimicked the movements of the two men, took a draw of smoke from the pipe, coughed once and handed the pipe to Walkara who sat it down at his feet.

"Why have you chosen my daughter as your mate?" asked Walkara in a monotone voice that bordered on anger.

"Well, I guess we kinda chose each other. When I first met her when she was tendin' to the boy, I thought she was mighty pretty. But I think it was 'cause she was a strong woman, strong enough to be a match for me. Ain't never met a woman like that. We just hit it off right away."

"Hit it off?" asked Lame Deer.

"Yeah, you know, we just seemed to like each other right off."

"She is a big woman, a strong woman, most men have been shamed by her when she proved to be a better warrior or hunter. Why does that not shame you?" asked Walkara.

"Probably cuz I'm bigger, and stronger, and ain't much of nuthin' gonna shame me. I'm glad she's big and strong and a good warrior. I want someone that can fight right beside me."

The two men looked at one another and at Reuben and stood. With an outstretched arm Walkara said, "Big Bear, you may have my daughter as your woman. I ask that you keep her safe and let her have many children. If she does right, love her. If she does wrong, beat her. Make her a good woman."

Reuben was a little surprised at the 'beat her' expression but he extended his arm to clasp forearms with Walkara and again with Lame Deer before they stepped aside to let him exit the wickiup. Spotted Owl was seated outside the wickiup near the remains of the cook fire and jumped to her feet as Reuben ducked his head and exited the lodge. He smiled when he spotted her and she knew her father had accepted him. She ran to him and jumped up like a little girl and clapped her hands as she looked at Reuben and asked, "What'd he say, what'd he say?"

"He said I was s'posed to beat you!" he said sternly.

Spotted Owl froze in place and a look of fear covered her face as she looked at Reuben who couldn't keep his stern look long and broke into a smile as he said, "He welcomed me into the family!"

Spotted Owl slipped her arms around his waist and hugged her man and laughed and looked up at him and smiled. As they walked back to the wickiup Reuben asked, "Ain't there some kind of ceremony or something that we're supposed to do become husband and wife?"

"Yes, you just did it," she declared. "But there is one more thing, I must welcome you into our lodge," she said as she smiled up at her choice of a mate. They arrived at the wickiup and Brewster was lounging outside by the cook-fire seated on a large stone, his walking stick on the ground beside him. Reuben looked at Brewster, down at Owl and back at Brewster and said to the boy, "Uh, Brewster, you need to get your stuff outta the wickiup."

"Oh, we gonna go back to the cabins?"

"Uh, not exactly, you're gonna throw your blankets in the trees yonder for tonight and we'll be leavin' in the mornin'," instructed Reuben.

With a confused expression on his face, Brewster said, "But I don't understand, I thought you were sleepin' in the woods."

"I was, but ya' see, me'n Spotted Owl went an' got married, so, uh, you know," stuttered the big man.

Brewster raised his head and looked at Reuben as a smile began to spread across his face and he replied, "Oh, now I get it. O.K. then, but we're goin' home in the mornin'?"

"Yup, in the mornin'," declared Reuben.

The big man assisted Brewster in gathering his things and making his temporary camp in the trees in the same place that Reuben had bunked the night before. Brewster looked at his friend and said, "I sure am happy for you Reuben, she's gonna be a perfect wife for you. She's a good woman, yessir, a real good woman."

"I think so too. I never thought about marryin' up before, but it just seemed right with her. Her Pap, he called me Big Bear, said he expects us to have lots of young'uns."

Brewster chuckled as he looked at Reuben, "Big Bear, that sure fits, an' I bet the two of you outgrow yore cabin in no time a'tall."

When Reuben returned to the wickiup, Spotted Owl stood at the doorway looking more beautiful than Reuben thought possible for any woman to look. Arrayed in a white tanned dress that reached just below her knees, the long fringe that draped across the yoke, down the sleeves and at the hem of the skirt was adorned with tiny bells and blue and white beads with tufts of fur at the very end of each piece of fringe. Across the yoke was a row of the ivory bugler teeth of elk that gleamed white as they hung from braided bits of bright blue deerskin. The entire yoke was adorned with an intricate pattern of porcupine quills and blue and white trade beads that showed a diamond pattern within a circle. Her hair hung in braids that were interlaced with blue and white ribbon and tufts of white rabbit fur. Her smile betrayed a touch of timidity that was unusual in a woman of such confidence but was becoming nonetheless. Reuben's heart beat so strongly and loudly that he thought it was about to jump out of his chest, but his weak knees threatened to give out as he walked toward his bride. She stretched out her hand to welcome him to their home. He ducked his head and turned his shoulders to squeeze through the small doorway as she dropped the blanket behind them.

It was a beautiful evening as the brilliant sunset seemed to color the entire world with its gold. Even the deep black timber held the gold on the tips of their needles and the usual black shadows cradled the colors at their breasts treasuring the last moments of the day. Clancy held the cup of tea as it rested on her belly while she listened to the talk between the women and Caleb as they shared memories of childhood. Looking at the edge of the timber, Clancy leaned a bit to the left to see a little better, then recognizing the big form of Reuben she leaned forward and saw there were three riders with four horses and one horse was pulling a travois. She jumped to her feet, set her cup on the rail, and began clapping her hands as she said, "They're here, and he brought her back! And Brewster too!"

The others on the porch stood to get a better look at the returning men and their guest and their pack. Caleb flashed a knowing smile as he recognized Spotted Owl and the grin on Reuben's face told the story. He stepped off the porch as they reined their horses to a stop in front of the cabin and looking up at the big man he said, "Congratulations you two. I'll take care of the animals, you better go introduce your company to the women folk. They're anxious to meet your woman. Did you two get hitched proper?"

"We did that, her Pap did the customary thing. He's the chief you know, so it's proper according to their way so I guess that's good 'nuff."

Caleb lowered his voice and said, "Uh, that one woman up there's a missionary type so you might kinda step careful round her," he warned.

When he stepped onto the porch, Clancy did her best to hug the big man as she said, "I'm so happy for you Reuben, I knew you'd bring her home!" Her welcome set the big man at ease and pleased him immensely as he motioned for Spotted Owl to join him with the women. He began his introductions with, "Ladies, I want you to meet my wife, Spotted Owl." He was surprised when both the Barbaras gave him broad smiles and eagerly accepted his outstretched hand as they congratulated him and his new wife.

THE LENGTHENING SHADOWS OF DUSK TOLD Jeremiah it was time to find a campsite for the evening. He turned to Laughing Waters and nodded his head toward a cut in the timber that beckoned them toward a small clearing that bordered the spring fed stream. As the woman motioned to the clearing the boy that rode at her side quickly reined his horse into the opening and explored the site for their night's camp. Little John had proven himself to be a skilled horseman that seemed to have been born on horseback the way he instinctively connected with any horse he straddled. Only ten summers old, he had already proven his skills with a horse, a bow and a rifle were equal to many twice his age. His broad smile at his mother showed his approval of the chosen campsite as he dismounted and took the reins from his mother so he could tend to both their mounts. His father, Jeremiah, would tend to the pack horse and his own mount. With ample daylight left Little John asked, "Are we going to hunt for our supper Father?"

"Oh, I don't know, we might look around a bit, see if we can scare up some fresh meat," then turning to Waters he asked, "that be all right with you? We'll get you some wood 'fore we go." She nodded her head in acceptance of his offer although it was usually the woman's job to get the firewood when they were in the village, but she enjoyed the way of the white men and especially her husband when he sought to help her at every opportunity. Within her village she was the Shaman of her people and many of the village tended to her needs in exchange for her services as the Shaman or healer and spiritual leader. Even though she was the spiritual leader of her people, she knew Jesus as her Savior and had little difficulty sharing the truth of Christianity with her people. She never contradicted their beliefs regarding the Great Spirit for she believed the Great Spirit to be her people's name for the one true God as told about in the Bible. She was proud of her husband and his consistent faith in Christ and his example of life that he lived before their people. His example made it easier for her people to believe when she told them about Christ. She smiled as her son Little John followed in the footsteps of Jeremiah in every possible way including his faith in the Lord. As she looked at Little John her mind went to fond memories of both Caleb and Clancy, the two young people adopted by Jeremiah and Waters. Caleb had been the step son of Jeremiah's sister that her husband brought back with him from Michigan and she naturally took him under her wing after she and Jeremiah were married. Clancy had been rescued by Jeremiah and Caleb after a Crow war party wiped out the wagon train that Clancy's family was traveling with and Clancy was the only survivor. When Jeremiah brought her back to their lodge, Water's heart melted at the sight of the waif with flaming red hair and she immediately took her in her arms and their hearts were knit together instantly. It was a special joy when the two of them were wed. It was the possibility of a new child that prompted this journey of Jeremiah and Waters to see the two wandering children.

The clatter of the falling firewood brought Waters out of her reverie and she looked at her husband as he said, "We're gonna take a little walk around 'n see if we can find any fresh meat. We won't be gone long. If we don't shoot anything, we'll see if we can get some fish from those beaver ponds back yonder." She nodded her head and started toward the packs to fetch her cooking utensils and the supplies necessary. She knew her man would want some coffee when he returned so she set the coffee pot aside as she dug through the packs.

The last several days of travel had been through the mostly flat plains that held little but buffalo grass, cactus, scattered clumps of pinion, juniper and cedar with fleet footed antelope and coyote. Now that they were in the hillier type country with mesas, plateaus and more trees, they were optimistic about their chances of downing a fat mule deer that would be coming down to water in the creek. It was in the latter part of daylight the deer would sneak out of their feeding areas and expose themselves to find the much needed water. The two hunters carefully made their way along the base of a towering escarpment of granite that stretched to the top of the flat mesa above them as they sought a good promontory that would give them a view of the water below. Their camp was behind them about two hundred yards and well hidden in the deep draw between the two plateaus that sheltered it from sight.

Jeremiah knew that just to the South of their present location was the narrow valley that held the Cherokee trail that would continue to the West and eventually meet up with the Oregon trail. It was a wide declivity along which the trail had been cut before it broke out of the mesa country to the Sweetwater basin. The two hunkered down behind a sizable boulder that was obviously a broken off piece of granite that at sometime in the past had stood upright against the mesa like the many other pieces that shouldered together at the escarpment and surrounding crown of the mesa. Jeremiah noticed movement to his right and he recognized it as a couple of mule deer that were picking their way through the scattered rocks to find a path to the water. He waited to see how long it would be before Little John spotted the game and he turned to see the boy was already watching them. Quietly Jeremiah motioned for the boy to use his bow instead of the rifle knowing the bow would require them to move closer to the game. As the deer worked their way down the slope, Little John was visually marking the path he would take for his stalk. Slowly he rose from behind the boulder and carefully placing his steps he moved at an angle toward the deer being careful to stay hidden behind the intervening boulders and scrub brush. Jeremiah stayed behind to watch and his pride grew as the boy moved with grace and stealth that would be the envy of any hunter. The boy took his time and moved only when the deer were focused on their goal of the water below. After about fifty yards, the boy paused, lifted his bow and pulled the arrow back to its length, held it as he sighted along the shaft and when the trailing buck hesitated in his step the boy let fly the missile of death. The whisper was barely heard and not alarming as the deer's only movement was the quick jump after he was impaled through the heart with the arrow. The sudden jump lifted the deer completely free of the ground but it was dead before his hooves touched soil again and he fell in a clump while his companion fled through the scattered juniper and disappeared.

"Aiiiieeee!" shouted the boy as he jumped over the boulders and ran to the side of the downed buck. He turned and looked back at his father and raised both arms and shouted again, "Aiiiieeeee! We have meat tonite!" Jeremiah grinned ear to ear as he trotted down the slope dodging the strewn stones and made his way to the side of his son. He was proud of this young man and he didn't hesitate to show it. "You did fine, son, real fine. I'm proud of you!" he declared. "But now the work starts," he said as he unsheathed his Bowie knife and bent to the task before him. Little John lay his bow to the side and with his own knife started the skinning process at the foreleg of the deer. Suddenly a distant sound that resembled rolling thunder stopped their work as the two froze in their movement to better listen. Jeremiah turned to look to the South but the shoulder of the big butte restricted his view but he knew the sound was more distant than the nearby hillside. He recognized the sound as gunfire and that much of it meant there was some kind of battle going on and with so much gunfire that probably meant a wagon train was under attack.

He turned back to the carcass and his son and said, "Let's get this done and get back to camp. There might be trouble comin'," said Jeremiah with a frown furrowing his brow. Before the dusk turned to sunset and the West was painted with color, the two hunters were back in camp. When they returned the expression on Water's face told Jeremiah she heard the gunfire as well and she now questioned his thinking. "I'm thinking it's a wagon train, but I don't know what's goin' on, maybe some Cheyenne, they've been on the prowl lately, or it could be a bunch of renegades. I just don't know. Let's get our cookin' done and put out the fire, maybe move camp and we'll wait till tomorrow to check it out. There was so much shootin' goin' on there had to be quite a bunch of 'em whoever they were and they were too far away for me to be of any help, so tomorrow will have to do."

Being even more careful than before, the trio of travelers worked their way through the maze of upthrust buttes and plateaus that were sprinkled with clusters of juniper and cedar. The occasional stunted pinion and sagebrush added little variety to the landscape but only hindered the making of a trail. Jeremiah led the way as he trailed the packhorse behind him and worked his way up a slight shoulder that jutted out from the escarpment around a large mesa. Stopping and dismounting he moved at a crouch to view the scene in the valley beyond. After surveying the entire area for any movement, he turned and motioned for Waters and Little John to come forward bringing his mount and the pack horse. As he mounted he said, "It's a terrible sight, but we gotta check things out. There might be somebody still alive." His grim expression warned his wife what to expect and she steeled herself and looked to her son knowing it was not going to be a good experience but he needed to learn.

The wagon train had circled and set up defenses but were apparently overpowered and outnumbered. All the wagons had been set afire and were nothing more than smoking embers and ashes with steel wheel rings and other wagon parts remaining to identify what the pieces had once been. Bits of harness and trace chains with bone and hair told of slaughtered horses while blood soaked rags told of the remains of people that fought to the last moments of their lives. Shattered dreams were scattered with windblown torn pages from books and bibles with family trees inscribed that told of entire families that died. Bodies were strewn askew and mutilated with clothing ripped from their bloody frames and heads crowned with blood where scalps had been taken. Buzzards circled overhead while wolves, coyotes and ravens tore at what little flesh remained on the carcasses of animal and human alike. Jeremiah had dismounted and walked from the remains of one wagon to another and looked upon body after body to see if there was any sign of life. There was none. Anything and everything of value or use had been stripped from the wagons and the bodies leaving nothing behind to identify anyone. There was nothing they could do.

"Should we bury 'em Pa?" asked Little John.

"No son, there's too many of them. 'sides if we did, and the Cheyenne were to come back and see they were buried, they'd take after us and do the same to us. There's too many of them and too few of us. We best get a move on."

Having already determined the attackers were Cheyenne by the remains of the broken arrows and lances and that they had left to the West, Jeremiah knew they were probably just tending to their dead and wounded and would probably come back this direction. He knew their primary territory was to the East and North of this location but he also knew that at this time of year they were known to travel any direction and any distance for their raids for horses and women and vengeance on any white man. After he mounted up he looked back to the West and motioned to his small entourage to move away to the South in the direction of the distant mountains and their goal of the Medicine Bow Range and the home site of Caleb and Clancy.

The last thing he wanted to do was to bring a rampaging raiding party of Cheyenne down on his unsuspecting family in their new home. It was still early in the day and they had a good day's travel before them, they might even be able to make it to the new cabin before dark. Just the thought of seeing Caleb and Clancy again brought a big smile to the face of the buckskin mountain man and as Laughing Waters looked at her husband, she knew exactly what he was thinking and she smiled in agreement.

THE PORCH HAD BECOME THE FAVORITE GATHERING place for both the beginning and closing of each day. The colors of the dawn and sunset combined with the aroma and taste of fresh brewed coffee and the camaraderie of good friends made each day a treasure to be held and cherished. The ladies were seated, Clancy in her rocking chair and the two Barbaras in the ladderbacks while the men leaned against the railing or squatted against the logs except Caleb and Brewster that shared the split log bench. Long moments of quiet were comfortable among friends and shared laughter brought smiles to everyone. Clancy looked at the youngest of the group and asked Brewster, "I bet you were pretty scared when that Grizzly stood up on the trail, weren't you?"

"Boy howdy, if my horse hadn't reared up and dumped me o'er back'rds, I'd prob'ly jumped off an' lit out afoot, I was so skeert. I knowed I could outrun anything 'bout then," he chuckled as he remembered.

"But wasn't it after you got dumped that you were injured?" asked Clancy.

"Yes'm," and he paused, remembering, then in a lower voice he said, "and you know, when I was tumblin' down that hill I thought sure I was gonna be kilt. If the fall didn't do it, I thought sure that ol' bear was gonna come after me, an' you know, just before ever' thing went dark, I remember thinkin' how scary it was not knowin' for sure what was gonna happen next. You know, if I was gonna make it to Heaven or . . . the other place."

"You mean you don't know?" asked Clancy quietly. Everyone had become still and very attentive, some concerned and others interested.

"Uh, no m'am. I was orphaned when I was real young and had to make do on my own since I was knee high to a grasshopper an' ain't nobody ever told me 'bout it," replied Brewster somewhat embarrassed.

"Would you like me to tell you, or perhaps Caleb?"

"Would you m'am? I'd like that."

"Of course, I'll tell you just like I was told . . . it's really quite simple. You see, the first thing you need to know is that we're all sinners, you understand that don't you?"

"Oh yeah, m'am, I know that."

"And God says in the book of Romans chapter 6 and verse 23 that what we deserve because we're sinners is death. Now that's not just dying, because everybody dies, but the price for our sin is death and hell forever. Do you understand, Brewster?"

"Uh, I think so m'am, but I don't want to go to hell."

"And that's the good news, when Jesus went to the cross and died there, he paid the price of sin for us so we don't have to and then He also says in chapter 10 and verse 13 *For whosoever shall call upon the name of the Lord shall be saved,"* explained Clancy.

"What's that mean, call?" asked the interested young man.

"That just means to ask God in prayer to save you from that penalty of sin, or hell."

"You mean that's all I've got to do is just ask?" replied Brewster with a surprised look on his face.

Clancy smiled as she answered, "I told you it was simple. But you have to mean it with all your heart. You can't just say it because you want to get out of trouble, you have to believe it with all your heart. You see, Brewster, when Jesus paid the price for our sin He purchased the gift of eternal life for us as a gift and that's what we ask God for, that gift of eternal life to be saved from the penalty of hell. But you must believe it with all your heart."

Brewster dropped his head and thought about what he heard and looked up at Clancy and said, "But I'm not sure I know how to pray and ask, will you help me?"

"Of course I will, but before we do," she looked around at the others and asked, "what about everyone else? Do each of you know Christ as your Savior, have you accepted the gift of eternal life?" and she looked from one to the other. As she looked at the brothers, they smiled and Chance spoke for the two of them, "Our folks taught us about the Lord from the time we was first walkin' and we both accepted the Lord." She looked at Reuben and he said, "Yes'm, my mammy tol' me 'bout the Lord an' made sure all of us little'uns accepted that gift 'fore she passed on." Clancy let her eyes rest on Spotted Owl and the woman said, "I have always believed in the Great Spirit and He has always guided me in my life."

Clancy looked back at Brewster and said, "I'll start us in prayer," and lifting her voice so all could hear, she added, "and if anyone wants to be sure then just say this simple prayer in your heart with us. And Brewster, just follow along and say this same prayer to the Lord. *Dear Jesus, I ask your forgiveness for my sin and I ask you for the gift of eternal life you promised in your word. Guide me from now on, in Jesus name, Amen.*"

She lifted her head and looked at Brewster and saw a broad smile on his face and knew the burden that he carried for so long was gone. She stretched out her arms and he came to her for a good old fashioned momma hug. Reuben had respectfully turned his back to the rest and looked across the clearing and down to the valley below them and noticing movement he said quietly, "I think we got visitors comin', looks like . . . three people, a man, woman, and youngster, and four horses. Don't think it's trouble but . . ."

Caleb stood and stepped to the rail to shade his eyes and look down the trail at the approaching group. A smile began to spread across his face and he turned to Clancy and said, "It's Ma and Pa and Little John." The announcement brought Clancy to her feet, however slowly, and she pushed her way to the rail to watch the arrival of the long awaited family. She stretched her arm as high as she could reach and started waving and bouncing on her toes and her excitement was spreading to the rest of the group. Reuben said to the others, "We might need to make room, I'm not sure this porch is gonna hold us all."

Caleb helped Clancy down the steps as Jeremiah and Waters drew near and shouts of welcome were exchanged. Little John was the first on the ground and ran to the waiting arms of his big brother and the two hugged like a couple of bear cubs and slapped one another on the back and laughed. "Boy, have you grown! Why you was only this high," with an outstretched hand at waist level, "when we left, an' now look atchu! You're darn near as tall as I am." That was a slight exaggeration as Little John was a good head shorter than his brother but he was tall for his age. He was outfitted in buckskins and the resemblance to his father was evident, his dark complexion came from his mother and both parents had coal black hair, but the facial features and the broadening shoulders and lanky frame showed his father's lineage. Jeremiah now stood beside his sons and when Caleb turned he was met with a bear hug from Jeremiah that was so tight he was gasping for air when released. Although Caleb had become a sizeable man his father was still the larger of the two but the bond between the two was evident. Clancy was still held in the embrace of Laughing Waters as the two were laughing at the difficulty of hugging with the sizable obstruction between them. Clancy said, "Well, c'mon you two, we've got people for you to meet," as she pulled Waters toward the steps of the porch.

The waiting group had parted to make room for the newcomers and with broad smiles the introductions were made all around. It was a happy time and the crowded porch made the reunion all the more welcoming. The two Barbaras assumed the part of hostesses and refilled the coffee cups and brought out some slices of fresh baked cake to share to everyone's delight. Jeremiah said, "You've got quite a settlement started here, next thing you know, you're gonna have a town goin'," as he waved his hand toward the valley.

"I was beginnin' to think the same thing. As much as I don't like town livin', we'll at least have a bit of a settlement. Reuben's buildin' hisself a cabin yonder," motioning with his chin, "and the ladies were plannin' on joinin' up with the next wagon train that came through, but I'm thinkin' they might be considerin' stayin'," he said as he looked toward the widows now seated on the bench. They smiled noncommittally. "They were part of a wagon train that left outta here a couple days ago and wanted to stay and help Clancy out, just in case you didn't make it, Ma, and they have certainly been a welcome blessing to us too."

Jeremiah looked at the two women and asked, "You were with a wagon train that came through here this past week?"

"Yessir, we were. Jedediah McAlllister's the wagon-master and he told us there would probably be another train through before too long if we wanted to join up and follow. We made good friends on the train but we thought we would be more help here with Clancy," shared Barbara Sparger with a smile.

"Uh . . . I don't know rightly know how to tell you this, but you need to thank the Lord you stayed on here," started Jeremiah but was interrupted by a disturbed Barbara.

"What do you mean, you're scaring me, Mr. Jeremiah," said Mrs. Brown.

"We came across that train early this morning. They had been attacked by a large raiding party of Cheyenne yesterday and the entire train was wiped out."

Both women caught their breath with their hands to their mouths and said, "Oh Lord no! Did anyone . . ." they started to question but Jeremiah dropped his gaze as he shook his head no.

"Oh those poor souls, and the children, oh my, my, my," then looking at Jeremiah, Mrs. Sparger said, "You're right, Mr. Jeremiah, we must thank our Lord for bringing us here. Oh my," she said as the two women hugged one another to give consolation. The others just watched and remembered their brief encounter with the passing wagon train. Spotted Owl's eyes lowered into a slight squint and her lips were drawn tight as she clinched her fists. Reuben watched her reaction and put his arm around his bride and drew her near in understanding. It was the Cheyenne that attacked her village and killed her mother as a young Spotted Owl watched.

The sad news sufficed to break up the gathering and the men dispersed to the upper cabin. Reuben and Spotted Owl had set up her hide teepee in a nearby clearing a short walk from the main cabin while the widows had made themselves comfortable in their wagon. The loft over the bedroom in the main cabin would be taken by Jeremiah and Waters while Little John would spread his blanket on the floor before the fireplace. Accommodations were comfortable all around and everyone looked forward to a good night's rest before beginning a very busy day on the morrow.

BY ANY STANDARD OF MEASUREMENT JACKSON Bubash was an old man and his chosen get-up contributed to that image. A floppy grey hat pinned up on one side blended with his long silver hair that hung with slight curls to his shoulders. His whiskery face was groomed and combed to a point at his chin where his chin whiskers brought order to his sideburns and trailing moustache. Bushy eyebrows did little to hide his piercing black eyes and his skin held surprisingly few wrinkles. A long fringed jacket with strips of beading that dropped from each shoulder to the pocket flaps that offered the only color to his attire. Gambler striped britches were tucked into high topped moccasins that held matching beading on the toe pieces. His unusual attire matched his flamboyant and confident character as the scout of the first ever cattle drive to cut a swath through the middle of the Rocky Mountains and disputed territory that was sometimes claimed by what would later be the territories of Utah, Kansas, Nebraska and Texas. One of the few men that knew this country, he had been chosen for his knowledge and not his temperament and he accepted because of his boredom with the flatlands of central Texas. His only excitement there was roping armadillos, shooting horn toads, and teaching his daughter everything there was to know about cows, horses and men.

His daughter, Marylyn, had proven herself to be a better hand with horses than any man he ever rode with, and a better drover than Charles Goodnight or his partner Oliver Loving that according to Jackson didn't know which end of the cow had a tail and which had horns. "Ain't neither one o' them been weaned from their momma's milk yet no how." When Margaret Heffernan Borland told him about her brother wanting to take a herd to the Medicine Bow Mountains in the territories to start a ranch and supply the wagon trains that were going on the Oregon Trail, he told her she was "crazier than an ole' houn' dog!" to attempt such a thing. But he knew she was of tough Irish stock and Jackson had known her first husband, Harrison Dunbar. Jackson also knew her second husband, Milton Hardy, and her third husband, Alexander Borland. It was because of her assistance that Borland had been able to start his cattle empire that after his death she continued to build. So Jackson knew her determination and he thought if anybody could do it she could, and if anyone got in her way, she'd probably plow them under. When she offered him the job as scout, he decided it would be better than wasting away roping armadillos.

So it was that Jackson Bubash made his way back to the campfire of the drovers as the dusk lost its grip on the last bit of sunlight and the sun settled itself behind the snow capped mountains in the West. The drive had taken over two months to reach this point, two months of blazing trail where a herd had never been driven and wagons had never rolled. The early days were easy compared to the last couple of weeks, the flats of Texas and the disputed territories were without too many incidents. After they hit the Arkansas and moved West into the Bayou Salade, so called by John Fremont on his exploratory expeditions, they began to understand the challenges before them. But when they had to push the herd over Weston Pass and into the valley of the headwaters for the Arkansas, the Texicans realized what cold weather could do to a man, and that was in the late Spring. Moving through the broad North Park area was better and just the day before the crossing of the Colorado gave them quite a time, what with losing well over twenty head to the muddy runoff waters. Now they were resting at the base of what Jackson had told them was the last bit of mountains they had to cross before they would drop into the valley of the Medicine Bow Mountains. As Jackson found himself a seat near the fire, he scraped a spoonful of beans and salt pork from his plate and pushed it into his gaping mouth, just as James Heffernan started his usual whining questioning.

"I thought your job as a scout was to find the easiest way for us to go and all we've been doin' is goin' up and down mountains and across rivers and frankly I'm tired of it!" he exclaimed.

Jackson looked at the man and continued chewing his mouthful of beans and salt pork. When he finished he took a long draught of hot coffee and sat the cup down on a nearby stone and looked back at the complainer and slowly said, "It's still light enough, so take a look yonder at those mountains to the West there, what do you see?"

He swiveled on his seat and looked in the direction pointed and said, "Why mountains, of course."

"And what's on those mountains?"

He looked again, and back at Jackson as he snidely replied, "Snow."

"And those mountains yonder to the East?"

"Why snow, of course, but I don't understand," whined the man still attired in his britches, shoes with spats, white shirt under a waistcoat, and an ascot at his neck. Similar attire than what he had worn for the whole trip as he rode and bunked with the cook.

"Now, take a look back the way we came and then the direction we're headin'," said Jackson as he took another bite.

"And . . ." whined the man.

"Do you see any snow?" asked the old man.

"Well, no, I don't."

"So, does that make it easier goin' thataway than that direction?" he asked as he pointed to the West.

"Well, yes, I suppose."

"Then I guess I'm doin' my job," mumbled the old man as he took his last bite before cleaning his plate with the small morsel of corn biscuit. Without saying any more, the scout stood and left the fire to retire to his blankets. His grinning daughter watched her dad's figure fade into the twilight. The rest of the men held their laughter behind stifled snickers and almost in unison lifted their coffee cups for one last swallow before turning in for the night.

The well established routine of the morning was followed again as Jackson conferred with his daughter, Marylyn, before he left on his early scout. It was still dark but the silhouette of the Eastern mountains was outlined by the whisper of promised morning light. Marylyn was the designated wrangler for the remuda of horses and would start the herd as soon as there was light to see and because of the need for a trail cutter, one of the vaqueros, Candelario Lopez, would lead the way. The remuda of about 35 horses usually traveled about a half mile ahead of the herd and would make the trail easier for the herd to follow. Next would come the cook wagon, pulled by a four-up hitch of mules well ahead of the herd, for the cook would have to set up and have the noon meal ready by the time the drovers arrived for the mid-day break.

When the herd was ready to move the trail boss, Jeter Collett, took the lead or point because of being short-handed with one of the drovers helping with the remuda. Ashton Crocker, the number two man behind the trail boss, would be on the left flank and Candelario's brother, Manuel Lopez, would take the swing on the left. Two other vaqueros, Diego Martinez and Federico Garcia would take similar positions on the right. Usually there would be a couple of men that would take drag and be at the tail end of the herd to take care of any stragglers but they had lost one man during an attack by some Kiowa just before entering the territories and another was lost when his horse stepped into a prairie dog hole and threw his rider over his head and snapped his neck. But they had managed by having the two swing riders alternate their positions with the drag and picking up any stragglers.

Their scout had directed the drovers to move the herd along the East bank of the muddy river and follow it to its headwaters and cross their last obstacle of mountains through this cut. The sage and pinion gave way to scattered juniper and cedar and soon small groves of Aspen dotted the hillsides. This was a reasonable climb and the animals continued on their head swinging gait with occasional stops to grab a bite of buffalo grass or to nip a flower or two. After they crested the broad back hills, Marylyn motioned for Candy to head on back to the herd as she could take them through the park like areas that nestled between the thick green quakies or Aspen. She marveled at the beauty of the country with the leaves of the quakies waving in the slight but cool breeze and the clear azure blue of the sky. The rolling hills with the greenery and the distant snow capped peaks were sights she had never enjoyed before and she reveled in the magnificence of God's creation. She thought, *I'd sure like to live in this country. It's a whole passel prettier the flatlands back home, and we ain't got nothin' to go back to, that's for sure. I wonder if I could talk Pops into makin' us a home out here.*

As she was thinking about it, the horses broke into an open park and from the high meadow she found herself overlooking a long wide beautiful valley below. In the distance she could make out the deeper green of the river bottom and to her left the continuing range of mountains her Pop had said was the Sierra Madre. In the distance to her right was the granite peaks of the Medicine Bow Range and she knew they had arrived at the valley of the Medicine Bow, their goal. It would take another day, maybe two to make it all the way to the final stop, but they were here and it was beautiful. She spurred her horse to turn the herd back to the trees and get them to circle up and start to graze as they waited for the chuck wagon and the herd for the noon break. Within moments she had the remuda settled and she dismounted and dropped to the ground and stretched out her legs in the tall grass, laid back and spread her arms and gazed at the sky above and said, "Yes! This feels like home!"

Suddenly a voice behind her said, "Think so do ye?" and her father's face looked down at his daughter lying in the grass and she could see his smile through the bush of grey whiskers and said, "Yes, I do, Pops. This just feels like home! Even though I ain't never been here before, it just seems like I've seen it in my dreams or sumpin' cuz I love it! Can we stay? Huh? Can we?"

"Well, I don't know, we'll just have to think about it I reckon. We ain't got much to go back to that's for sure and it is right purty here," he said as he stood straight and gazed at the scenery spread before them. The creak of the wagon and the rattle of trace chains caught their attention as the chuck wagon pulled alongside the grove of Aspen and stopped. The cook and James Heffernan stepped down and Heffernan briskly walked to where Jackson waited. Noticing the direction of their gaze he glanced in that direction and stopped abruptly. He stood still and stared, captured by the same vista as the others and breathing deeply of the fresh air he smiled and turning to Jackson he asked, "Is this the valley?"

Jackson nodded, smiling, and replied, "Yep, but it'll probably take a week or so to get down yonder where we need to be goin' but we're here alright."

THE INTERVENING DAYS BETWEEN THE SHORT honeymoon and the present day were not wasted by Reuben and Owl. Every waking moment had been spent snaking out logs and skidding them to the location of their new cabin. Now the task of cutting timber and snaking logs had been taken over by a still limping Brewster but he was glad to be of some use. Although not as adept at felling the trees as his bigger friend, he prided himself in making the right choices and being able to drop the trees on his mark. Little John assisted Brewster by trimming the branches from the dropped logs. Caleb and the brothers were busy finishing the corrals and would probably join the building by late afternoon. Jeremiah was providing the needed brawn with Reuben in trimming, notching and lifting the logs at the site of the cabin, while Spotted Owl stayed busy with the many tasks of helping fetch the tools and give assistance when another hand was needed, which was often. It was a busy but happy bunch of hard working men and women.

Although Clancy's helpfulness was somewhat limited, Waters and the two Barbaras enjoyed getting acquainted around the preparation of the meal for the many workers and the cabin was filled with happy chatter.

Clancy had moved her rocking chair into the cabin and now sat with one hand on her tummy and the other dropped to her side to pet Rowdy who was flopped on his side with his tongue lolled out and enjoying the attention. Waters looked at the very pregnant woman and pictured the young girl that used to follow her through the woods as they searched for the many plants used in the natural remedies and cures. She had been an inquisitive and energetic girl as well as a quick learner both about the plants and the skills as a hunter. Waters remembered the girl's first kill on their elk hunt and how she had bested the men and boasted about it for several days after. The thought brought a smile to her face as she looked at the wistful woman stroking her pet. "I meant to tell you earlier, Two Bits passed over mid-winter this year. He was a good dog. Little John was very sad for a long time, they were best of friends."

The thought of her long time companion brought a tear to her eye as she replied, "I was afraid to ask. I knew he was getting very old, that's why we couldn't take him to St. Louis with us, but I'm glad he was a friend to Little John. When I got Rowdy here, it was because he reminded me of Two Bits, and I think he's going to be about as big too and he's become pretty protective already."

Waters turned to the other ladies and explained, "When we found her she had the biggest black dog, some even thought he was a bear, and he wouldn't let anybody near her. He was very protective, he even killed a Crow warrior that was trying to kill her and Caleb."

"Oh my! That is protective," said Mrs. Brown a little taken aback at the casual manner that Waters spoke of someone being killed, but she was beginning to understand the way of the wilderness and that life and death were almost an everyday occurrence.

"Clancy became quite the hunter herself, I was just thinking of the time she shot her first elk and how she bragged about it to the men for days afterwards."

Looking at the frail appearing but very pregnant woman in the rocking chair, Mrs. Sparger said, "You killed an elk, all by yourself?"

While Clancy nodded her head, Waters continued, "That's nothing, she killed a Grizzly bear right in front of their cabin as it was charging Caleb!"

Both women caught their breath and looked at a smiling Clancy as she tried unsuccessfully to appear a bit bashful or demure but broke out into laughter as she remembered the day. "The fur from that bear is in there on our bed if you wanna see it," she said.

Both women dropped what they were doing and trotted in to examine the thick fur on the bed. When they returned they almost stumbled over one another in their chatter as Mrs. Sparger said, "It's so huge!" and Mrs. Brown said, "It's so soft!" Waters and Clancy looked at the two women and giggled at their responses and Waters explained, "Out here, we do not let anything go to waste. That bear gave its life to keep them warm and it has done that."

The two Barbaras looked at one another and returned to their unfinished task of helping with the meal. Waters said to Clancy, "I think you can ring the bell to call the men to eat. It will be ready when they get here." Clancy rocked forward, pushed herself up and waddled to the door with Rowdy at her heels excitedly thinking he was going to go somewhere. Hanging from the eve at the edge of the porch was a large metal triangle with a nearby rod that was used for calling the men to meals or in the event of an emergency. It was one of those extra supplies that Caleb thought of when they were still in Independence and on their way West with the Buffalo Brigade. It would serve its purpose today.

The noontime chatter was focused on the progress for the day and most of that was concerned with the cabin. When asked about his part, Jeremiah said, "Well, we've got four almost five courses up on the walls and since Caleb and the boys are done with the corrals, we will probably be ready to start on the roof by mornin'," he surmised.

"My, you are making progress," interjected Mrs. Brown, "I thought it would take much longer than that to build a cabin."

"Well, I've built more'n my share and from the way Reuben's been doin', I'm thinkin' this buildin' is nuthin' new to him either," then turning to the big man he added, "Am I right Reuben?"

"Yessir, I've built a few in my day. But what we done with them hardwoods an' what we can do with this pine's a lot different. Why, them hardwoods we gotta split and plane an' everthin' but these Pine, why, all we gots to do is a bit a' shavin' an' some notchin' an' it's ready to go. Why, this is almost easy!" responded Reuben.

"If this is easy, I'd hate to have to work alongside you when you were doin' those hardwoods like you said," said Chance.

The cabin filled with laughter as everyone knew none of the men could keep up with Reuben when he was busy at any task, especially when his strength was an unparalleled tool.

What was easy for Reuben would be back breaking for the average man. And his stamina was also beyond compare. As the men finished their meal and were pushing back from the table, thanks were said all around and the ladies graciously accepted the compliments as they cleared the dishes and Waters re-filled the coffee cups.

"Chance, how 'bout you helpin' Brewster and Little John in the timber and I'll take Colton to the cabin site and help Reuben and Pa, that be all right with you?"

"Sure, I kinda figgered Brewster could use a break with the axe and mules. We can trade off and it'll be easier on both of us."

"Good thinkin', and don't forget we're gonna need some good tall ones that aren't too big for the ridge poles but they gotta be big enough to hold up the roof."

"Yeah, I know, like these," he said as he looked up at the ridge poles overhead that they used for the roof of the main cabin.

"That's right, like these would be just fine."

As they left the cabin the men went to the assigned job sites with Brewster, Chance and Little John taking the mules into the timber to snake out the trees and skid the logs to the cabin. Brewster pointed out the trees he marked for felling and the two walked through the timber sizing up additional trees for the ridge poles and wall logs. Returning to the last site of cutting, Brewster took up the axe and started on a sizeable tree that would make a good log for the lengthy side of the cabin. With three cuts for a notch, he walked to the back side of the tree, looked up at the top to re-examine the branches and the expected direction of the fall and began to make the cuts for the fall. Little John and Chance stood to the side with plenty of trees between the action and their location and watched as the now experienced Brewster wielded the sharp double bladed axe. With about eight or ten cuts, the tree started to lean and creak, Brewster stood back and looked up to watch what direction it would fall and yelled, "Timmmberrrr!" and watched and the big tree creaked, snapped the remaining portion of the trunk through and toppled with its branches catching other trees branches on the way down with a combination whisper and crackling before a ground shaking and dust raising thud announced the completed fell.

"Whoooeee and another one right on the mark! Good goin' Brewster! That's right where you said it'd go! And look, most of the branches done broke off!" shouted Little John.

"Just tryin' to make your job easier, Little John!" replied Brewster.

Brewster stood the axe against another tree as he walked Little John down the length of the fallen tree pointing out the branches and the spot where the top needed to be cut. While the two followed their routine Chance picked up the axe and started toward the next tree. He did a cursory examination of the trees height and branches and started making his preliminary cuts for the felling wedge. Brewster looked back at his friend and watched as he started his labor. From the distance, Brewster looked at the tree top and back at where Chance was making his cut and thought it might be all right but he would move to the side to be sure there wouldn't be any chance of getting hit by the falling tree. As Brewster looked back at where Little John was and where the mules were lazily grazing on bits of grass waiting to be put to work, Chance started on the back side and main cut on the tree. Each swing of the axe and strike of the blade to the solid wood of the tree trunk caused a resounding thunking sound that echoed throughout the timber and Brewster could tell by the sound that Chance was getting a good cut with each swing. Turning back to watch his friend at work, he looked up at the shaking tree top and back down along the shape and size of the large tree. What he was gauging was the weight and lean of the tree and the probable direction of the fall and what he saw was not what Chance was calculating. Brewster let out a shout at the same instant the axe struck wood and Chance didn't hear the warning, with another swing the axe bit deep and the tree started to topple but in the wrong direction. Brewster turned to Little John and yelled, "Little John, jump!" The big eyes of the young man immediately saw the falling tree as if it was in some dream but his reactions were with the quickness of youth and he dove alongside the large log he had been trimming just as the branches of the falling tree peeled other branches from the nearby trees and slapped the ground. The top of the tree spanked the rear of the team of mules that screamed a bray and leaped forward in an attempt to escape and launched themselves along the familiar path used to skid the trees. The last Brewster saw of them was the wave of grey tails and the echo of their startled braying. Brewster had jumped behind the nearest tree that was big enough to shield him and he was untouched.

Before the dust even settled, both Brewster and Chance were vaulting through the branches searching for Little John and desperately calling his name. "Little John, Little John, can you hear me?" called Brewster. Chance was closer since Brewster was still a little hindered by his game leg and he too called for the boy. Finally a weak, "Yeah, I'm here. I'm O.K. . . . I think," he replied, coughing in the dust. He was pushing aside the sappy branches of pine needles trying to find an escape from his entrapment. Finally his head stuck up and a dusty face smiled at the two searchers and said, "Boy, that was close!"

Chance walked along the trunk of the just felled tree and reached down to help the youngster up from his nest of pine needles and asked, "Are you all right? You're not hurt are you? I'm sorry, I thought sure that tree'd fall the other direction, I don't know what happened."

"Ah, that's all right," said Little John.

"Sometimes they can fool ya', I thought you were cuttin' it right, but when I looked at it from back yonder I saw the heavy branches on the other side and tried to warn ya' but you couldn't hear me, so I warned Little

John just in time. Ya just never know 'bout 'em," said Brewster. "You wanna go get the mules back and I'll cut the next one?"

Chance nodded his head in the affirmative and started down the trail in pursuit of the fleeing mules knowing he would have to explain to the others what happened. *Dumb mules anyway, why'd they have to run off.*

JACKSON BUBASH WAS THE FIRST MAN AT THE cook's fire for his cup of coffee. He was always surprised how quietly the cook moved and did his work of a morning what with the metal pots, pans, cups and everything else that naturally tended to noise. Somehow the cook managed to get the huge pot of coffee boiling over the smoldering flames as it hung from the tripod without any of the usual clattering noise that disturbed the cattle or the men. Two big partially buried dutch ovens were under a mound of hot coals and Jackson's mouth watered at the thought of the hot biscuits with honey butter dripping as he tried to smash the entire biscuit into his mouth. This promised to be the last day on the trail and Jackson savored the early morning with the cows still, horses unmoving and cowboys snoring almost in harmony. He sat on a grey log alongside the fire and looked across the orange glow as he watched the hunkered back and elbows of the busy cook at the back of the chuck wagon. Cooky, Jackson didn't know his real name, had done a fine job of taking care of his duties for the entire drive and Jackson couldn't remember a drive or a time he'd enjoyed the same cooking more. There had been as much variety as possible and always ample servings and very few complaints from the men.

The scout looked over near the rope corral that kept the horses nearby and saw the prone form of his daughter stirring from her blankets. His blankets still lay mussed beside her and she sat up and rubbed her eyes as she looked in the direction of the fire. With a wave of her hand, she slipped on her vest, her hat and stepped into her boots before making her morning trek to the trees. She soon joined her Pa at the fire and accepted the proffered cup of coffee. Seating herself beside him she asked, "So, this the last day of the drive?"

"Yup, reckon so, we'll probly get the cattle down to the mouth of the valley round mid-day or so, that's where the cabins're 'sposed to be and the corrals an' such. From what Heffernan says he thinks his partner's gonna want some of us to hang around an' sorta show 'em the ropes about cows an' all. Reckon none of 'em ever done any cowboyin' afore."

"So, who's gonna be stayin'?"

"Well, you was talkin' 'bout wantin' to stay round these parts. Think you could teach some greenhorns 'bout cows an' such?"

She looked at her Pa as if he had lost his mind or something and looking down she shook her head and replied, "I could teach, but could they learn? Not too many fellers take to learnin' much about cowboyin' from a woman. But I would like to stay. How many fellers they got?"

"I don't know 'bout that an' don't know nuthin' 'bout the ones they do have, but I'm thinkin' we'll be findin' out 'fore the day's over."

As Jackson and Marylyn were finishing their coffee the other hands made their way to the circle and poured themselves some java and seated themselves to wait for their breakfast. Usually the herd would be on the move by this time, but with a short drive and being the last day, Jeter Collett was letting everyone take it easy. As they waited, James Heffernan came to the group and asked Jeter, "Did you say anything about what we spoke about last evening?"

"Uh, no, I thought I'd let you ask 'em if you're of a mind to, Mr. Heffernan," replied Collett.

James nodded his head and said, "When I spoke to my partner, Caleb Thompsett, in St. Louis, he knew he would not have experienced cow hands and asked if it would be possible for some of you to stay on and work or at least stay on and help his workers to learn a little about how to handle cattle. Would any of you be interested?" he asked as he looked from man to man. The four vaqueros looked at one another and nodded at Candelario, Candy, to speak for them. He stood up and said, "We have made plans that as soon as we are done with this drive, we are going to California. We have some family out there that have asked us to help them on a big rancho that has many thousands of cattle and horses and they need some help. We promised we would come and help them. Also, this country is too cold for us." The four vaqueros smiled and enthusiastically nodded their heads as Candy sat back down and retrieved his coffee.

James looked at Ashton Crocker, the right hand man to Jeter, and with raised eyebrows asked if he would stay. Crocker looked at Marylyn and said, "Well, I was hopin' a certain little woman would be interested in seein' things my way and comin' back to Texas with me and be my woman, but she's been all fired stubborn, so, no, I don't think I'd be interested in stayin'."

"Well, that leaves you, Jackson and your daughter of course, I don't suppose you'd want to stay in this cold country would you?"

"As a matter of fact, Mr. Heffernan, my little girl here and I were just talkin' 'bout that and I think we just might like to give it a try. If'n it don't work out, I'm sure we can always find our way back to Texas if'n we want to, but for now, yeah, we'll stay on a spell."

"Great, great, I'm sure Caleb will be happy to hear that. And that takes a lot off my mind. I was afraid if no one else stayed, I would have to stay and instruct his men, but thankfully I won't have to, so thank you Mr. Bubash, and you too Miss Bubash."

All the men had to either duck their heads or turn aside at his mention of his instructing anyone about how to handle cattle or horses, since he rode in the chuck wagon all the way from Texas and refused to dirty his hands on any of the usual chores of a cowboy. He repeatedly complained about the 'stinking cows' and the trials of the drive. They all would be glad to be away from his sniveling ways.

By the time breakfast was over, Marylyn was well on

the way down the valley with the remuda. She was very skilled with the horses and she attributed much of her ability with the animals to her skill with a long black snake bull whip. Like most cowboys from down south she carried a riata tied to the saddle strings in front of her right knee, but behind her leg and tethered to the saddle strings behind her, when not in her hand, was her ever present bull whip. When she uncoiled the twenty five foot length of the braided black snake leather with the flat snapper on the end, and brought it back in its big arc by the time it went forward she could crack it almost as loud as a rifle shot. All the horses recognized that sound and would immediately respond by turning away from the crack and as a result, Marylyn could handle the herd with ease. The men of the drive had grown to respect the woman and her skill with the whip and with the animals as well. Now she moved them steadily into the tall grass at the bottom of the valley and to the trail alongside the North Platte. Within sight of the horses, the chuck wagon followed in its jaunty fashion with all the creaks and rattles as it sought out the trail. Just breaking from the trees on the widened trail was the first of the herd that had spent the night in a broad park on a slight shoulder of the timbered Sierra Madre range.

Lame Deer and Horse Killer were back in the black timber out of sight of the girl and Cooky. Lying prone on a promontory that overlooked the valley, the two warriors watched the activity of the drovers as the herd slowly came into view. Without movement they waited until the entire herd passed then slowly they returned to their horses and mounted to follow. Their scouts had spotted the herd four days ago when they approached the Sierra Madre near the Muddy River and now Lame Deer's responsibility was to follow the herd until they stopped and report back to Walkara. Now the two scouts stayed far back in the trees and made their surveillance one of listening rather than watching. As the drive continued into the late morning Lame Deer noticed a slowing of pace and he and Horse Killer again tethered their mounts and moved closer under the cover of the trees and the thicker scrub oak brush. It was evident from the movement of the animals this was the destination of the drive. The log fencing nearby indicated some structure for the animals and others were there and waiting. When Lame Deer spotted Reuben or Big Bear as he was known to the people, he knew his sister would be nearby and he moved to see if he could locate her. Looking back at the edge of trees he saw some other activity that prompted him to work his way farther into the trees and around toward what he determined was a lodge being built. There sitting on a pile of logs, watching the men below in the valley with the cattle, was his sister, Spotted Owl. He quickly mimicked the call of a magpie and she looked his direction instantly recognizing his call. She ran to the trees and spotting him as he stepped from behind the trees, she ran to him and greeted him, "Greetings my brother. What brings you here?"

"Our father asked us to follow these men and they have come here. What is this?" he asked as he motioned toward the herd of cattle.

"The men with my husband are starting what they call a cattle ranch. They will raise these cattle and sell them to other settlers that travel through. He says they are good to eat."

"Waaghhh, they will drive away the game from the valley!"

"He says no, they will live with the elk and the antelope and even the buffalo," she argued and continued, "he also says that when winter comes and our people cannot find meat, he will give our people some cattle for meat."

The surprised look on Lame Deer's face told of his doubt and even disbelief but he did not question her, he knew it was not the way of their people to lie. But he wondered about the white man or even the black white man. "I will take this to our father."

Spotted Owl touched her brother on his arm and pointed behind her as she said, "My man is making a big lodge for us. Will you and my father come when it is finished?"

"I will tell him but I cannot speak for him."

She dropped her eyes and dropped her hand from his arm, then looking back up at him she said, "It is good to see you my brother. My lodge will always be open to you."

He rested his hand on her shoulder and turned away. With a motion of his hand to Horse Killer the two went to their horses, mounted and rode quickly but silently away.

THE CRACK OF THE BULL WHIP ECHOED ACROSS THE valley and startled the workers on Reuben's cabin. The sound was as loud as but distinctly different from a rifle shot and as they looked in the direction of the report another crack split the stillness of the valley. Then the herd of horses came into view as they trotted along the trail bunched together about four or five abreast. At first sight, Caleb and company thought mustangs, but that didn't explain the loud report. They looked for any give-away as a source of the disturbance and in the slight dust cloud that trailed the horses appeared a single rider moving side to side herding the animals and keeping them totally in control. "Look at that wrangler handle them horses, ain't that sumpin'?" asked Chance as he straightened up from his work at notching one of the ridge logs for the cabin.

The rest of the men moved to the corner of the cabin that was nearest the valley floor and watched the approach of the horses. Another movement in the distance showed the canvas bonnet of the chuck wagon and Caleb knew the herd had arrived. He removed his hat and wiped his brow as he turned to the cabin crew and said, "Fellas, that's the remuda for the herd. The cattle we been expectin' are followin' the chuck wagon yonder so we probly' oughta walk on down there and make them fellers welcome."

Chance continued to watch the wrangler behind the horses and marveled at the use of the whip and the way the horses were so easily controlled. He looked from the horses to the wrangler and back again and continued to watch as he moved to follow the others to walk to the valley floor where the greetings and introductions were to be made.

Marylyn Bubash had fashioned herself a couple of leather split skirts for the drive from Texas. She first saw the skirts when a visiting neighbor arrived at their place sitting astride her horse but still wearing a skirt. Marylyn was amazed and pleased at the possibilities. She had always had to don men's britches to ride astride and tolerate the accusations of tomboy although she never considered herself such. But with the split skirt she didn't have to forego any of her femininity, at least in her own mind, and could still have the ability to more easily handle any animal she chose to ride. The leather skirts had proven their worth on the trail drive and now she gave little thought to them as her normal attire, but she realized they might be new and even startling to someone more accustomed to the side saddle type of riding. Riding behind the herd of horses she concentrated on the animals as she saw the corrals before her but she also saw the gates were closed although there were several men sitting on the rails and watching. She cracked her whip, put two fingers in her mouth and let loose an ear piercing whistle and with a motion of her uplifted hand the men got the message and one jumped down to open the gate. With just a couple of cracks of the whip and some deft reining she quickly maneuvered the animals into the nearest corral and reined aside as the blonde headed man standing by the gate watched. She motioned for him to shut the gate and he stood and stared. Finally he said, "You're a girl!"

"That's right, but if you don't shut the gate you're gonna get run over!"

Chance dropped his eyes to the gate, to the circling horses in the corral, and back to the girl and quickly moved to shut the gate before the horses circled back his direction. Marylyn reined her horse to the fence, dismounted and flipped the reins over the top rail, then mounting the top rail to be seated and watch back up the valley she took off her floppy felt hat letting her long blonde hair fall to her shoulders and shook it out, ran her fingers through it and replaced her hat. She looked at Chance as he stepped on the bottom rail and up to seat himself on the top rail about two feet to the side of Marylyn grinning all the time.

"Howdy, and welcome," he thrust out his hand and offered to shake, "my name's Chance and . . ." looking around he spotted his brother walking in his direction, ". . . that fella comin' thisaway is my brother Colton. Say, that was some doin', the way you handled them horses. I ain't never seen the like."

"Thanks, I've been doin' it purt' near all my life, so it comes pretty easy. I'm Marylyn, Marylyn Bubash. My Pa's the scout for this outfit. Are you two," nodding toward Colton, "part of the ranch set-up here?"

"Yeah, reckon we are, we came with Caleb and Clancy from St. Louis. We were part of the Buffalo Brigade, but when Caleb offered us the chance to come with them we liked the idea and signed on with 'em. Glad we did, they're good folks."

The get acquainted party of the two was interrupted with the arrival of the herd with all the accompanying activity and noise. The drovers had let the cattle amble slowly and now in the deep grass it took little effort for the herd to circle up and start grazing. The chuck wagon pulled near the corrals and was setting up to start preparations for their slightly delayed noon meal. The drovers rode to the corrals and tied their animals to the rails, loosened the cinches and made sure they had enough lead to graze, then the men walked to the chuck wagon to await a hot cup of fresh coffee.

Caleb, Jeremiah and Reuben walked around the corrals and headed to the chuck wagon knowing the men they sought would undoubtedly be near the coffee pot as well. When they approached they were hailed by James Heffernan with an enthusiastic, "Caleb! Boy it's good to see you! We made it, as you can see. We started off with just over a thousand head and last count showed we had nine hundred five. That's not bad for a two and a half month seven hundred mile drive!"

"Yessir, yessir, it is good to see you. I didn't really expect you quite this soon but we're glad you're here. I see your cook is getting your meal ready but how 'bout you joinin' us at the cabin for the evening meal? I'm sure Clancy would like to see you as well. Oh, and by the way, this is my father, Jeremiah Thompsett," and as Jeremiah reached out his hand to shake, Caleb continued, ". . . and this is one of our partners, Reuben Caine," motioning toward Reuben. James frowned and hesitantly extended his hand to Reuben. His reaction was not missed by anyone but overlooked by everyone and the introductions continued to include the trail boss, Collett, and the scout, Jackson Bubash. Caleb also introduced the three younger men as 'partners' to the chagrin of Heffernan. Caleb and the rest were surprised when Chance introduced Marylyn and expressed their surprise not just at a woman with the drive but at her observed skill with the horses. When Heffernan informed them she and her father had agreed to stay on Chance was thrilled and everyone else was pleased as well.

Upon hearing they were going to be staying, Chance offered to take the afternoon and show her around the area, an invitation she gladly accepted. When Caleb learned of their plans, he begrudgingly allowed the brothers who had been working pretty steadily and deserved a little time off. When Clancy heard of the plans she watched the brothers hurry through their meal and race each other to the corral to saddle their horses for the afternoon ride. Caleb stepped to the porch and reminded them, "Be sure to take your rifles and pistols and be on the watch. I don't think we have to be concerned about the Ute but those Cheyenne could turn back on us and become a problem. And if you see some meat on the hoof, bring it home. We'll have company for a while and could use the extra meat." The boys nodded their agreement and tied off their mounts as they went to retrieve their weapons and gear.

They walked their horses to the corral in an effort not to appear too anxious and casually reined them next to the girl's mount. Stepping to the ground the brothers tethered their mounts and climbed to the top rail to await their guest. They looked at one another and Colton said, "She's quite a looker ain't she, Chance?"

"Yeah, she is, Colt, but don't forget, I saw her first."

Colton chuckled as he looked at his brother and said, "I know, I'm just comin' along to keep you in line. I could tell right away you were taken by her. I don't mind, you are the oldest anyway and she's pretty old from the looks of it." A droll expression covered his face as he looked at his brother. Chance responded with a fist to his shoulder and said, "She ain't either, I bet she ain't no older'n me."

Marylyn walked up without the boys seeing her and saw the scuffle but saw it was in good natured fun and asked, "Now what are you two fussin' about?"

Colton piped up with, "We were tryin' to guess your age, Chance said you weren't as old as he is and I said you were. So, which one of us wins?"

"Uh, don't you fellas know it ain't proper to talk about a woman's age?"

"It ain't?" asked Colton.

"No, it ain't! Didn't your Momma teach you any manners?" asked Marylyn.

Both boy's expressions sobered and Chance quietly said, "Our folks died a while back and before that we didn't have much of a chance to learn any kind of manners. We've pretty much had to make do on our own." Then lifting his eyes to hers he let a smile stretch across his face and said, "But, we're willing to learn if you're willing to teach us!"

She smiled back at the two and thought to herself, *And here I thought there wouldn't be any man willing to learn from a woman.* Then she said, "You're asking a lot aren't you? I just got here and you're supposed to be showing me around, so let's get going," as she mounted up and reined her horse away from the corral. The brothers quickly followed to begin the quick tour of the nearby country and the area that would compose the ranch. The rest of the afternoon saw the three cover the nearby country with highlights of the hot springs, the foothills of the Medicine Bow viewed from a promontory on the saddle crossed over when they first arrived, the mouth of the valley and the wide vistas into the great plains, and the nearby Sierra Madre. They finished the tour when they returned to the cabins and the building of the new cabin.

While they rode the brothers were concerned with the scenery, locations of specials happenings like the buffalo hunt and the wolf pack attack, sites for the cabins and corrals. But Marylyn was observing the smaller valleys and ravines, the hidden areas with deep grass for graze, hazards that could endanger the cattle, hideouts for bear or cougar that would attack the cattle and other places of concern always with the cattle and horses in mind.

"Mr. Heffernan said there were some mustang herds

around this part of the country, where would they be?" asked Marylyn.

"We've seen some out past the mouth of the valley in the plains area. They seem to like the wide open spaces more'n the timber or the closed in valleys," replied Chance.

"Have you had any trouble from bears or cougars?" she asked.

"Not any trouble to speak of, a Grizz did spook Brewster's horse but she run off after that."

"A Grizz?"

"Yeah, a Grizzly bear. They're a lot bigger'n anything they got down in Texas. They're 'bout ten feet tall when they stand up on their hind legs and their fur's long and brown, and their head's big 'nuff to put a horse's head in their mouth."

The three were walking side by side toward the cabin while they talked and Marylyn stopped and looked at them, sure they weren't serious and said, "You're joshin' me, aren't you?"

"No m'am, we wouldn't do that. Tell you what, we'll see if Momma C will let you see her Grizzly bear blanket and you can see for yourself."

"Blanket?"

"Come on . . ." they said as they moved up the steps of the porch.

There were so many crowded in the cabin for the evening meal, the younger group consisting of Brewster, the Threet brothers, Little John and Marylyn were moved to the porch while the rest made room at the table for the evening meal. After Caleb asked the Lord's blessing, everyone served themselves and found a seat either at the table or nearby and the conversation flowed freely. On the porch Marylyn again expressed her amazement at the size of the Grizzly and more so that it was killed by Clancy. Chance said, "Well, you are in the company of some very special women. Clancy is just one of them, her Ma, Laughing Waters is a Shaman with the Arapaho people and Reuben's wife, Spotted Owl is a respected warrior and daughter of the chief of the Ute people. Mrs. Brown's husband was a pastor and missionary and she was headed West to do the same and Mrs. Sparger's husband was a doctor and she's carryin' on where he left off. Now here you come along and you're more of a cowboy and a wrangler than most men and you're about to teach us greenhorns how to handle cattle and horses as well as make a home for yourself in this wide open wilderness. Now, that sounds like a mighty impressive bunch of women, you included."

She looked at Chance and a small tear formed in the corner of her eye as she realized no man had ever shown her that kind of respect nor given her that kind of praise and she was moved by it. She had been attracted to this man when she first saw him but tried to pass it off as curiosity but maybe it was more than that. He seemed to measure up as more of a man than she originally thought although most men when compared to her father came up short, but Chance appeared to be different, better than most.

The conversation at the table centered on the herd and the plans for the future as both Heffernan and Collett spoke of the challenges of establishing a ranch under usual conditions and how it would be even more difficult in this wilderness. Caleb and Jeremiah began to read both the men as being pretty shallow when it came to facing difficult challenges and when Heffernan finally said, "So, I'm thinking I might take you up on your offer, Caleb."

"My offer, and just what offer are you referring to, James?" asked Caleb.

"When you said if our partnership didn't suit either one of us, the other would buy out," explained the whiney city boy.

"Oh, and what you're saying is you want to go back to Texas and forget about a partnership, is that it?"

"Yes, this country is not for me. We had some experience with the cold, and it is so isolated, no, it's definitely not for me," explained James. Caleb noticed Collett nodding his head and trying to obscure his smile with his hand.

"And just what were you thinking as to the price for the herd?"

"Well, at the market . . ." he started and the two men stood and walked outside to stroll around the cabin and discuss their business in private. It was just a short while when they returned and Caleb went into the bedroom and came out with two leather pouches. He emptied the pouches on the table, counted out forty lead balls and placed them all into one pouch and the remainder in the other. Handing the pouch to James he said, "There you go, paid in full."

He looked at Caleb with surprise on his face and said,

"What do you mean, these are nothing but lead balls like those for a rifle. These aren't worth anything!"

"Let me show you something," said Caleb as he reached into the pouch and extracted one of the balls. Pulling his big Bowie knife from its scabbard, he held a ball in the palm of his left hand and scratched a small portion of the lead from the surface of the ball exposing a gleaming gold ball beneath. "Each one of those are solid gold and weigh at least eight ounces. The forty balls will more than cover the amount we agreed upon and they are a very safe way to transport that much wealth." James smiled and shook his head, "I should have known to never doubt you my friend. We will be leaving in the morning and I wish you the best of luck." The two men shook hands and Heffernan and Collett exited together. Jackson Bubash stayed behind while his daughter continued to visit on the porch. Jackson said, "We like what we see here and if everything goes well, we might just stay, if that's all right."

"We'd be proud to have you, Jackson. I think you'll be an asset to our growing family." What Caleb didn't notice was the timid smiles exchanged between Jackson Bubash and Barbara Brown. However, those things are always noticed by the women that always have romance on their minds and Waters and Clancy smiled knowingly.

THE PROMISE OF THE NEW DAY WAS HERALDED WITH a banner of dusty pink painted across the Eastern sky as the sun made a stealthy appearance. Marylyn stood beside her buckskin looking over the saddle to her Pa as he spoke to the vaqueros. The Mexican men had high respect for the scout and tarried with their good-byes but mounted up as they said, "Vaya Con Dios compadre."

"And to you as well," responded Jackson, "an' if'n you ever get back thisaway, you fellers be sure to look me up an' if I'm still here you know you have a job with me." He tipped two fingers to the brim of his hat, nodded his head and turned away as the four men dug their big roweled spurs into their horses sides and took off at a lope on their way to California. As he looked at his daughter he said, "Those were some mighty fine fellas, yessir. I kinda hate ta see 'em go. But daughter, you n' me got some work ahead of us," but before he could get started he saw Heffernan and Collett and Cooky with the chuck wagon getting ready to pull out and thought he better speak to them before they left. Marylyn let her Pa say their good-byes and she waited patiently by her horse. From behind her came a voice, "I should just pack you up and take you with me anyway. Sometimes a man's gotta show a woman who's boss!" It was Ashton Crocker walking up behind her leading his horse, the big Roman nosed bay he always rode that no one else could get close to and didn't want to for fear of getting a hunk of hide taken. Marylyn moved to the opposite side of her horse to keep her mount between them and as she looked at the wall eyed bay she thought the horse and Ashton were a good match for one another, both mean and ugly plumb through. She answered his remark with, "Couple things wrong with what you just said Ashton. First, there ain't no way I'd let you just pack me up and you ain't man enough to be boss of me anyway!"

"I'll show you," he hissed as he dropped the reins of his horse and started around the buckskin after her. She quickly ducked under the neck of the buckskin and went to the left side of her mount regretting she left her bull whip still tethered on the opposite of the saddle. As Ashton continued his pursuit she started to move behind her horse but the mount of Crocker reached out with teeth bared trying to get a mouth full of skin which caused her to draw back into the arms of Ashton. He wrapped his arms around her waist and snarled, "Now I gotchu, you little wench, it's about time you gave in to me!" as he tried to turn her around to face him. She brought her left hand to his face and stuck her thumb into the edge of his eye causing him to yell, "You crazy . . .!" and loosen his grip which let her pull back, but his greater strength pulled her to him.

Suddenly a hand grabbed Ashton's shoulder and spun him around causing him to lose his grip on the girl and he faced the surprising new threat. Standing before him was the lean frame of Chance Threet but Ashton saw only the balled up fist at it collided with his face and knocked him back against the buckskin that spooked away causing the attacker to fall to the ground on his back with blood spurting from his flattened nose. He scrambled to get up but as he made it to his feet his eyes were blurred by the splattered blood from his nose and the image before him brought another right from the ground to the spot just above his belt and lifted him off the ground and robbed him of his breath. He doubled over and met a left hook to the side of his head that sent him to the ground with ears ringing and right eye swelling and the cut at his brow bleeding into his eyes. He sputtered into the dirt and tried to catch his breath but he hurt so bad he didn't think he could get up. He didn't understand what happened, it was all over in less than half a minute. Marylyn stood frozen as she watched the sudden onslaught of Chance and now as he stood with balled fists at his side and staring down at the vanquished woman attacker she again thought, as only a woman could, how good looking this man was.

The thought brought a smile to her face and she stepped to Chance's side and slowly put her hand on his arm and said, "Thank you, he's had that coming for a long time." She thought to herself. *But I wanted to give it to him with my bull whip but this is all right too, I guess.* Chance looked at her and bending down to pick up his hat he dusted off his britches and said, "No man should put his hands on a woman like that, my Momma taught me that. Are you O.K.?" he asked as he looked at Marylyn. She smiled and nodded her head as they watched Ashton struggle to his feet and stagger to his horse. He snatched up the reins and jerked them for the horse to follow as he walked toward the departing chuck wagon. He mounted the horse and dug his heels in and trotted off to catch up with the others.

"What was that all about?" asked Jackson as he came back to his daughter's side. He nodded at Chance as he waited for an answer.

"Oh, Ashton needed to have a misunderstanding straightened out and Chance explained things to him so he could understand," said Marylyn as she smiled at her Pa and back at Chance.

Jackson looked from Marylyn to Chance and back again knowing there was more to what happened but he accepted her explanation for now. "Well, we need to plan out what we're goin' to do to get these fellas lined out with these cows and such, don't ya think?"

It was decided that Jackson would take Caleb and Brewster and Marylyn would take the brothers and they would work around the cattle and the different draws and meadows and plan out the grazing and cutting of hay for the winter. That would leave Jeremiah and Laughing Waters to help Reuben and Spotted Owl to finish up with the cabin while the two Barbaras would tend to Clancy.

The valley of the North Platte or the Medicine Bow Range was as wide as fifteen miles in places but the chosen area for the ranch nestled in a wide horse shoe bend of the river and sat back against the foothills of the Medicine Bow. It was a fertile valley and the grass grew tall and the North Platte provided a good barrier to keep the cattle contained. If need be and the summer graze was good they could always push the herd across the river into the broader expanse of the valley, but there should be plenty of graze between the river and the timber. Come winter time the timber would be a good wind break for the animals and they could make a lean-to barn to store some hay for the deep snow days. As Jackson and Marylyn made the drive through the valley their experienced eyes noted right off that this country could support a much larger herd than what they had brought up from Texas. This bunch would be a good start but there would be no limit to the number of animals this country could handle. Jackson told Marylyn that the tall grass and wide meadows they passed through could easily support 100,000 or more cattle and that could be just the start. "This is good cattle country," he told his daughter.

While Jackson toured the countryside with Caleb and Brewster he pointed out the wide spring fed draws that had good tall grass that could be cut for the winter and other areas that the cattle could be moved into for additional graze. "As long as you keep an eye on 'em an' don't let 'em eat the grass down, move 'em around to give the grass a chance to recover, you should have good graze all year. Then in the winter, when the wind blows the snow clear, they can still get to some of the grass down in the valley and when they can't you can feed 'em up near the trees."

Whenever they were near the cattle Jackson would shake out a loop with his riata and give a quick lesson on roping the cattle and even show them how to heel the cows. "That's only when you got somebody else with a rope on their horns an' you need to stretch 'em out for brandin' or sumpin'," he explained. "It takes a lot o' practice to get handy with a riata, or rope, whatever ya' got. But, with practice, it'll come to ya'," he explained. "Mrs. Heffernan, she's smarter'n most when it comes ta' cows. All these she sent up here she had ol' Collet keep separated from the bulls 'till we got here so them cows won't be calvin' till Spring. Most o' them fellers back in Texas don't think 'bout that an' just let 'em have at it and they end up calvin' purty much year round. But Mrs. Heffernan knew the winters up here were purty hard so she tol' her brother and Collett to keep them bulls separate and they sure had a time gettin' them vaqueros to do it, but they done 'er."

Marylyn spent the day giving the brothers lessons with their riatas having appropriated the Mexican braided rawhide riatas from the other drovers and the vaqueros knowing they could easily replace them. Both boys took to the use of the ropes with ease and were readily roping the cows but the heeling was a little more challenging. Marylyn had a good day's entertainment as she watched the frustration of the brothers when they became entangled with the riatas wrapped around their heads and shoulders. She also instructed them about the pasture grasses and the need for cutting some of the grass for winter feed, although this was not a normal practice in the flatlands of Texas but she knew the winters in the mountains would be more difficult for the cattle.

As the day drew to a close, everyone gathered at the main cabin for the evening meal as prepared by the two Barbaras with Clancy pitching in as best she could. Once again, the younger group took to the porch to leave room at the table for the rest of the extended family and Caleb asked Jeremiah to ask the Lord's blessing on the meal and to bless the growing extended family of the Medicine Bow Ranch. It was a short prayer and everyone filled their plates and took their places as the usual chatter spilled over the table interjected with laughter and happiness. Spotted Owl stood back beside Laughing Waters as the two women looked at the crowd and at each other, Spotted Owl said, "At another time we would be enemies, but now you are my sister. I am glad for this."

Waters grinned and answered, "I am too Spotted Owl, you make me glad to have you as my sister. I also have another sister, her name is Pine Leaf, she is a war leader of the Crow and the mate of my brother, Broken Shield who is the leader of the Arapaho."

Spotted Owl looked at Waters in disbelief as she said, "A Crow war leader? Your brother is the chief of the Arapaho and he has a Crow war leader as his woman? This is hard to believe." Waters just smiled at her as she replied, "Yes, at one time the Arapaho were enemies with the Crow and now we are not, at least not our two bands.

And we were also enemies with the Ute, and now we are not, we are sisters. The Creator has done great things, has He not?"

"Yes, yes, He has, great things," she answered contemplatively.

THE LOOP OF THE RIATA SNAKED OUT AND DROPPED in front of Chance as he walked toward the main cabin, he skipped to the side to avoid the loop and continuing the swing of his own loop turned and dropped it over the head of his brother as he tried to coil up his own riata for another try at his brother. As the loop settled over his shoulders, Chance pulled the slack and the loop tightened around the arms of Colton and prevented him from retrieving his riata for his attempt at retribution. Both boys laughed at the game and Brewster laughed at both of them as he walked past them and said, "Keep him hog tied Chance, that'll leave more breakfast for me!" It was the start of another day and things were settling into a routine. With the newest cabin finished and Reuben and Owl moved in, Jackson and Marylyn had taken advantage of the invite of Owl to use the teepee until other arrangements could be made for the newest additions to the growing settlement.

Jeremiah and Laughing Waters had extended their stay due to Clancy's stubbornness regarding the coming birth as she grew and waddled around counting the days until she didn't know when. The two Barbaras were seriously considering making Medicine Bow their permanent home and were contemplating the best location for a cabin so one could be built before cold weather came calling. They too were anxiously awaiting the arrival of the newest member of the Thompsett clan. Today would be another day of focused instruction for the apprentice cowboys and this day would include Reuben and Spotted Owl. Caleb wanted to hang out a little closer to the cabin and was doing his best to come up with an acceptable excuse. The magnet of breakfast was drawing everyone to the main cabin and the different paths to the clearing and hide lodge held hungry and yawning folks walking toward the delightful aromas. The early morning sunlight cast long shadows from the pines but the smiles on the faces and cheery greetings stayed any remaining darkness.

The last to arrive was Jackson and the fringed jacket of the old man was just entering the doorway when the sudden clatter of hooves and the hollering of men caused the old man to whirl around with his sidearm in hand. Before he squeezed down on the big Walker Colt, he recognized Candelario Lopez and pulled up his pistol re-holstering it as he took the steps two at a time to the clearing. The four vaqueros slid their mounts to a stop in the dirt and were dismounting as the rear hooves of the horses skidded to a stop. All were excitedly trying to talk at once but Candy motioned them to be quiet and he said, "Senor Jackson, Indians, Cheyenne I theenk, many of them and they are coming thees way!"

Caleb and Jeremiah was right behind Jackson and heard the report and Caleb said, "How many?"

"Thirty, maybe more, they all had face paint!"

"What makes you think they're coming here?" asked Jeremiah.

"There were lots of tracks of wagons that came from this valley when the ground was wet and muddy. We were camped in a ravine by a mesa and we watched a small group of them looking at the tracks. Their ponies also were painted and we could see scalps in the manes, yellow hair, red hair and more. One of them pointed toward the valley and they went back. We thought they left but then we saw they were coming back with more. We agreed we needed to come warn you."

Jeremiah looked at Caleb and said, "Probably the same bunch that jumped the wagon train. They must have gone farther on the trail and raided others and now they're on their way back. Those tracks in the mud are a dead giveaway. We need to get ready."

By this time all the others from the cabin had gathered around and heard the report from the vaqueros. No one spoke, all waiting for Caleb and Jeremiah to set up a plan for defense. Caleb said, "Ladies," referring to the two Barbaras especially, "why don't you finish puttin' breakfast together, I know we could all use some coffee at least, and we'll figger out what's gonna be the best way to take care of things." He motioned to Jeremiah, Jackson

and Reuben to join him by the corrals. He told the
brothers and Brewster to gather up the rifles and powder
and shot and such and bring it to the porch and told the
vaqueros to tie off their mounts and get some hot coffee.

The four men at the corral had more experience at
fighting than all the rest. Although Reuben had little
experience with Indians, he was included in the group of
leaders. Jeremiah said, "First off, we need to calculate the
probable route of attack and the numbers of our defenders. They have us outnumbered, but I think we have 'em
outgunned."

"Yeah, and I think if we can make 'em think we don't
know they're comin' we could turn the tables on 'em too,"
added Jackson.

As the men looked and thought about the impending
attack they walked to the edge of the clearing to get a
good look at the valley below. They had the advantage of
the river before them and the timber around them with a
fall back of the cabins. As they looked and thought, they
strolled back and forth and finally returned to the porch.
Standing and leaning against the porch were the four
vaqueros, the two brothers and Brewster. On the porch
were Laughing Waters, Marylyn, Clancy and the two
Barbaras. Reuben looked around for Spotted Owl and
didn't see her, then looking at Waters he asked, "Owl?"

"She said there was something she had to do and not
to worry, she'll be back."

He nodded his head and looked down the trail in the
direction of his cabin and back to the men as they began
to share their planned strategy. Before they began, Caleb

said, "Just a minute Pa, I've got something for you," and went into the cabin. When he returned he held a piece of buckskin wrapped around something that he handed to Jeremiah. The man looked at his son and accepted the offered gift. He could tell by the heft it was a rifle but as he let the buckskin fall, he was surprised to see a new Sharps rifle. "I picked that up in St. Louis when I got mine. I've been waitin' for a good time to give it to you. This seemed like a pretty good time. I'll show you all about it in a bit, but first let's get things situated."

"Well this explains why you said you and me would be out yonder to give them their first welcome," said Jeremiah with a broadening smile on his face. He had heard of the Sharps and knew he would have to get one at the first opportunity. What had impressed him about the rifle was what he had been told about the range and accuracy. In the hands of a marksman, the rifle could down a buffalo at six to seven hundred yards, some even said a thousand yards, and that was more than double the range of a typical Hawken or other percussion rifle. The vaqueros all had India Pattern Carbines like those used by the Mexican troops that stormed the Alamo and the weapons were very deadly when loaded 'buck and ball' with .35 caliber buckshot in the .65 caliber Tercerlos rifles. With these rifles, Jeremiah and Caleb determined to use them at closer quarters. The brothers, Brewster, Reuben and the women all had Hawkens and would be stationed in good cover where their marksmanship and the range of the rifles would be best used.

The initial contact would be dealt with by Caleb and

Jeremiah who would have the greatest range and accuracy and could keep the Cheyenne at a greater distance. Jackson would coordinate all the activity as the attack progressed and Caleb and Jeremiah would have mounts ready to fall back and join the others. Now it was a matter of taking up their positions but first things first, and that meant breakfast and coffee.

When the rest of the men went to the cabin to eat, Reuben took off down the trail looking for Spotted Owl. He returned shortly evidently upset and said, "She done took off, her horse is gone an' so's her bow n' stuff. I don' know what she's up to an' it concerns me some," shaking his head but looking to Caleb and Jeremiah as if they could give him an answer. Caleb said, "She knows this country better'n any of us an' she's been takin' care of herself for a mighty long time. I'm sure she knows what she's doin' and she didn't wanna worry you none, so I'm thinking you'd do yourself and everybody else best if you buckle down and try not to worry none."

Jeremiah went to the big man and put a hand on his shoulder and said, "How 'bout you and me just step over here and have a quick prayer for her and all." Reuben looked at Jeremiah and nodded his head and turned with him to move away from the crowd. The two men had grown close to one another working alongside each other as they built Reuben's cabin and the mutual respect gave confidence to Reuben as he willingly shared the quiet moment with Jeremiah.

With breakfast quickly done Caleb began sharing the basic plan with the others. As they understood their part, they gathered up the necessary weapons and gear and started for their assigned locations. Each one would need to prepare their cover and firing platform according to their comfort and abilities as well as their part in the plan. None would stay in their position long and each would need a path of escape to retreat to their second or fall back position. Everyone was to remain under cover and out of sight as Jackson moved the cattle farther up into the draw or notch between the foothills and timbered shoulders that held the cabins. He was to be a decoy of sorts to give the Cheyenne the impression they were not expected and the residents of the area were going on with normal activities and would be caught by surprise. Everyone had been told to take with them ample supplies of water and food to prevent any unnecessary movement that would give away their position. It would be a tedious waiting game with no certainty as to when the Cheyenne would come and with what force or exactly in what manner or area they would attack. Jackson would be the only one mounted and he was expected to give the alarm at first sight of any approaching Cheyenne.

In the cabin, the women thought their best course of action would be to take some time in prayer and Barbara Brown was chosen to lead them in their entreaty to the Lord. As she poured out her heart before God, she was disturbed by the whining of the pesky Rowdy. He had been pacing the floor whimpering and walking to Clancy's chair, to the door, back to Clancy and around the table and back to Clancy, whimpering and whining all the while. Mrs. Sparger looked at the dog and up at Clancy and noticed the girl moving side to side in the chair as if she was trying to get comfortable. Barbara

Sparger stood and went to the far wall to a small table and secured her husband's doctor's bag and returned to the side of the rocking chair and the very uncomfortable Clancy. She used the stethoscope and put it to Clancy's tummy and listened, looked at her face and smiled and said, "It's time, isn't it?"

THE SLOW MOVING CLOUD COVER PROVIDED SOME relief from the usual glaring mid day sun for the arrayed defenders. On the broad stone promontory of the Northern most finger of timbered hills Caleb had taken a prone position that overlooked the broad flat plains at the mouth of the valley. Below him was the winding North Platte with the scattered willows and tall grasses at its banks. He knew that Reuben had found a shoulder with a cluster of boulders below him and to the left where he anchored the line of vaqueros that were stationed along the bank of the North Platte. Even from this elevated position Caleb found it difficult to spot the four men. About two hundred yards South was another ridge coming from the timbered Medicine Bow Mountains and he knew his father would be well hidden within those trees and outcroppings. He also knew Waters would be below him and somewhere between Jeremiah and the vaqueros to anchor the South end of their firing line. Behind him and in the open grassy meadow was Jackson idly moving his mount to and fro to keep the cattle away from the river and grazing farther back into the draw. Occasionally Jackson would dismount and keeping his horse before him he would lay a telescope across the seat of his saddle and scan the wide plains where the marauding Cheyenne were expected to appear.

The rolling plains stretched across the mouth of the valley a distance of close to fifteen miles. To the North lay the wide Great Divide Basin but the terrain beyond the North Platte was similar in its rolling character and was scattered with clusters of sage and juniper and pinion. Farther beyond rose the flat top mesas with the granite escarpments and rugged ravines that provided shelter to the many inhabitants of the plains. All of this also provided cover for the natives that became a part of their surroundings. But these Cheyenne had not explored the valley of the Platte and did not know who or what inhabited this country. Although they knew the wagon train came through this valley and they were aware of the Cherokee trail, their only thought at present was the possibility of another prey and more plunder in the form of more white settlers with their wagons.

Caleb was the first to spot the movement of the large war party, he turned and sounded his warning with the perfect mimic of a meadowlark and after a short pause he gave the low throated call of a dove four times. The trill of the meadowlark was to tell of the sighting and the four times call of the dove was to tell how many he saw with each call to indicate ten. The warning told Jeremiah there were forty warriors coming. Caleb also knew even though the war party was moving in the open, there would be an advance scout or scouts that would be hidden and his gaze continued to search for any sign of that scout. Caleb knew that every sense he had would be required and every skill he learned as a warrior for the Arapaho would be needed to find the advance scout. He watched for any small animal, bird, disturbed leaf or moving branch, bit of dust or anything slightly out of color or out of place. He also knew it would be his peripheral vision that would detect what he sought. Slowly his eyes methodically moved never stopping always searching. There. He waited, not breathing, waiting. Again. At a slight drop off from a cluster of sage and at the base of the brush, the black hair of the scout darker than the shadow. Caleb watched as the scout moved closer and to his right. He was about a hundred yards beyond the river when he stopped behind another cluster. Caleb waited, he didn't want the scout to warn the party. Caleb wanted to have the element of surprise. As he watched the scout he realized the Cheyenne was watching Jackson and the cattle. After he carefully scanned the area, the scout turned and quickly moved out to return to the larger party. Caleb let out a long breath as he was relieved they were not spotted but he also knew the attack would soon come. He also thought it would not come from the entire party. Giving the scout time to put some distance behind him, Caleb gave another warning to Jeremiah.

When they came there were only eight but they were scattered among the sage and the tall buffalo grass. Thinking they could approach without detection, their horses were left behind in a draw out of sight. The defenders waited until the first of the attackers reached the far bank of the river and as they stood to drop into the water and cross, the vaqueros let loose with the Tercerlos loaded with buck and ball and the front four of the attackers were practically obliterated when the .35 caliber buckshot balls scattered and cut them down along with much of the willows and grass along the bank. The bodies of the attackers were thrown back into the grass and when the smoke cleared from the Mexican carbines there was no movement. From Caleb's promontory he spotted two forms crawling toward the bank and he quickly sighted in and his big Sharps boomed with the projectile hammering into the back of the prone figure almost driving him into the ground. Quickly reloading he continued to watch but before he saw anything he heard the Hawken below him thunder with authority as Reuben's marksmanship catapulted another attacker backwards from his crouched position in the willows. A lazy cloud of grey white smoke drifted from the near bank of the river as eyes scanned for movement and the only sound was from the gurgling water laughing its way downstream. The stillness was broken with the roar from another Hawken that lay over the saddle of Jackson's well trained horse and the lead ball pierced the chest of one more attacker that hid in the willows. Still they watched and waited. There was no more movement from the opposite bank of the river, and Caleb scanned the plains. The war party was nowhere to be seen. He knew they could easily be obscured in any number of draws, ravines or depressions and they would be rallying to determine what the next action would be, but he also knew they would not leave without retaliation and what they would believe to be a sure victory and the prize of the horse herd that was spotted by their scouts.

Although their positions were now known, both Caleb and Jeremiah thought it best to remain where they were because of the advantage of the cover of the river and the encroaching timber and outcroppings. They didn't have long to wait. Suddenly the entire war party rose up from the depression and began their charge. Screaming and yelling their war cries with feathered lances waving over their heads the thirty plus warriors lay low on their mounts as they formed a wedge shaped charge. Caleb and Jeremiah's Sharps barked almost simultaneously and two of the leading warriors were struck from their mounts to the surprise of the rest. But the fall of the two did not slow the rest as the onslaught continued.

With but short moments to wait until the charge was within range, the Hawkens of the second tier of defenders roared in a thick cloud of smoke and the entire front of attackers fell with several horses tumbling end over end. The screaming continued as arrows began to fly and the trade fusils roared from the mounted attackers. Again the Sharps found targets and two more bodies were launched from their mounts. The attack slowed and the riderless horses added confusion to the charge and as they neared the bank the buck and ball loaded carbines of the vaqueros roared in unison and the black wall of death claimed riders and horses alike as a blanket of blood was splattered on the grass and brush. The screamed shouts of the remaining leaders turned the attackers and they fled from the unexpected carnage.

There were still over twenty warriors that retreated with some laying on the necks of their horses obviously badly wounded.

Clancy was helped to her bed by the two women and as nurse Sparger tended to her patient, Mrs. Brown busied herself readying water, rags, blankets and anything else she could think of that might be needed. The pains were evident and Clancy struggled to find any degree of comfort. Mrs. Sparger reassured her as she said, "Everything's going to be fine, you're a good strong woman and I've done this many times. We'll just let nature take its course and trust the good Lord to work things out."

With an extended groan and her hand on her tummy, Clancy looked at Barbara and said, "Yeah, but the Cheyenne are comin'!"

"They're not coming here, they haven't been invited," proclaimed nurse Barbara.

"All the same, you just hang my pistol right here on the bedstead, just in case," insisted Clancy. Nurse Barbara looked in the direction Clancy pointed, walked over and picked the pistol and holster from the peg behind the door and hung it on the bedstead post near Clancy's head. The girl smiled and nodded her head as another pain started and the smile turned to a grimace.

The roar from the initial volley of the vaqueros to repel the first attack caused all the ladies to jump a bit and look toward the door. The concerned look on all their faces did little to reassure one another but they knew there were other concerns more pressing and the sudden cry that was forced from Clancy focused their attention on that more pressing issue.

The cloud cover had increased considerably and now the dark clouds were churning with a threat of a storm. In the mountains storms moved in and quickly let loose their wrath resulting in flash floods and lightning ignited fires that could cause untold devastation. Both Caleb and company and the Cheyenne knew the threat was nothing to take for granted and the best thing any of them could do was to find cover. Caleb knew a good heavy storm would keep the Cheyenne from attacking and the Cheyenne knew it could also provide cover for them to get nearer their quarry. It was late afternoon and the storm would probably continue into the night. When the storm broke, it broke with a vengeance and attacker and defender alike sought protection. Caleb and company quickly returned to the cabins for food and shelter and the Cheyenne sought protection on the lee side of the flat top mesas with the tree lined ravines.

The stomping feet on the porch startled the women and when the door was thrown open they let loose with screams. Caleb and Jeremiah were caught by surprise and pulled back quickly and saw they were the cause for alarm and then laughing they followed Waters into the cabin. What they were greeted with was more than a surprise as they saw Nurse Barbara at the side of Clancy in the bedroom. Barbara Brown went to the doorway and started to close the door, but admitted Laughing Waters before saying, "Excuse us gentlemen."

EXCLUDED FROM THE BEDROOM, CALEB BEGAN taking stock of the defenders. On the porch, he watched as two vaqueros helped to carry one of their companions to the porch. The fourth followed behind carrying the weapons of the others. Diego Martinez hung suspended between Candelario and Manuel Lopez and Federico Garcia carried the rifles. As they carefully sat their friend on the bench of the porch, Caleb saw the blood coming from his shoulder that bore a broken arrow shaft. Caleb went inside and summoned Waters, "Ma, one of the men has an arrow, can you take a look?" he said through the closed door. When she came out, Caleb asked, "Is Clancy O.K.?" with a worried expression on his face.

"She is doing fine, it is just the way it is with a woman," then looking around she asked, "and where is this man with the arrow?" Caleb motioned to the porch and she quickly went to the door. With a swift examination, she instructed the men to bring the wounded man inside and seat him at the table. Without any wasted movement she rested a knife with the blade in the fire, took a rag and dipped it in the hot water in the pot over the flames and began to clean the wound. She had already dismissed Caleb and directed Mrs. Brown to remove the man's shirt and jacket. Mrs. Brown was visibly disturbed by the sight but steeled herself against the blood and expected treatment so she could be of assistance to Waters. Marylyn had taken over as a helper to Nurse Sparger in the bedroom with Clancy.

While the women turned the cabin into a makeshift hospital, Caleb and Jeremiah were making the porch into the battle headquarters while the downpour splashed around them. Jackson Bubash remained below on lookout and would fire a round from his Hawken if any danger was perceived although none was expected. After reviewing the results of the day and the anticipation of another attack, it was agreed that if the storm let up in the night the Cheyenne would probably try to move closer before attacking at first light. Their discussion was repeatedly interrupted and punctuated by the rattle of thunder and the crack of lightning. Everyone was told to restock their powder and shot, get warm blankets and be prepared and as soon as the storm started to let up, they would return to their chosen locations.

While the storm continued to batter the mountains and the wind roar through the pines, the men on the porch had to raise their voices to be heard but their conversation was interrupted by a smaller but clearer voice from within. Immediately recognizing the cry of a baby, Caleb jumped from his seat and ran to and through the door to find Marylyn holding a tiny squealing form hidden in a bundle of blankets with little fingers waving at his daddy. Caleb stopped stock still and looked but was brought from his trance by a scream from Diego as Waters thrust the shaft of the arrow through his shoulder. The intact arrowhead had to be pushed through to be extracted and once through the wound would be dressed.

Caleb looked back to his son and walked slowly to Marylyn as she extended the child to his dad and said, "You have a fine son." Caleb looked at the woman, back to the child and then to Marylyn again and smiled as he took his son in his arms. Then almost as an afterthought, "Clancy? Is she alright?" Marylyn nodded, grinned and turned her back to return to the bedroom, leaving Caleb holding the child. As he looked down at his son he didn't notice the decreasing sound of the rain but stood swaying with the feather like weight of the boy in his arms. Jeremiah came in, saw Caleb with the bundle and smiling he approached Caleb and said, "Well congratulations son, what are you gonna name it?"

"It? It's a him! I have a son! Uh, . . . I don't know what we're gonna name him, we never really decided that, I don't think," he shared with confusion written on his face.

"Well, you better hand him off and come with me, the storm's lettin' up and we got a little matter of some Cheyenne to take care of come daylight."

The storm clouds moved off almost as quickly as they rolled in and a sliver of moon was joined by a smattering of stars in the black sky. Everyone was hunkered in place long before any hint of morning light made its appearance. Marylyn had brought a canteen of coffee wrapped in a thick fur blanket to provide some relief for her tough old man of a Pa and he gratefully accepted the offering. He had retreated to a stack of logs near the corner of the corral that held the horses, knowing the animals would be a prime target for the raiding Cheyenne. Caleb asked Marylyn to join her father near the horses and replaced her at the fall back line with Brewster. Again, the hardest part of the strategy for the battle was the waiting. The earlier confrontation had been handily won by the defenders but the next battle could just as easily have a totally different outcome. They were down one shooter with the wounded Diego still at the cabin, but Waters had left the women to tend to Clancy and had resumed her place at her husband's side. But even at nearly full strength, they would still be outnumbered by almost three to one.

As expected, the Cheyenne used the cover of darkness to remove their dead and wounded and also to take position closer to the river so their attack could be more easily mounted. The defenders had the advantage of the Eastern horizon at their back so that when any light came from the dawn, it would be behind them and in the face of any attackers and more revealing of any position in the brush or grass. Caleb's eyesight had adjusted well to the darkness and with what little light offered from the sliver of moon and the few stars, he was able to scan the terrain on the far side of the river. It was nothing but shadows and dim images, but he knew from his time with the Arapaho that often the shadowed images were actually the forms of the enemy camouflaging themselves with carried branches of sage and other brush. Movement was what he watched for, even the slightest sway of a shadow would be a giveaway. As he watched, several shadowy images slowly moved but never in tandem, always individually and very slowly. He knew there were many there in an area that was normally devoid of brush and held only sparse grass of even height, but now there was an abundance of bushes. With his mastery of bird calls he now turned in the direction of his father and sounded the night call of the Great Horned Owl. Watching the brush, he noted the movement stopped and nothing moved. He knew his call was perfect, he had earned his Arapaho name He Who Talks to the Wind, because no one was able to distinguish his calls from the actual calls of the animal. When the movement began again, he sounded his call again, knowing his father and the rest of the defenders would be ready for the soon coming attack.

But when it came, just as the first slice of grey lay on the horizon, they were surprised. The twenty warriors were now over twice that number. There were about twenty that had patiently crawled forward in the darkness and rose to launch a fusillade of arrows across the river into the brush that harbored the vaqueros and the rocks behind that held the brothers and others. But another twenty or more mounted warriors came screaming on horseback and added to the assault. The surprised vaqueros let loose with their cannonade of buck and ball and furiously reloaded as the second line of Hawken armed defenders began to pick at their targets. The noise of the screaming Cheyenne and the roar of the rifles against the few fusils of the attackers was like the roll of thunder of the night before. Caleb and Jeremiah took advantage of the greater range and accuracy of the Sharps and took their targets from the charging mounted warriors and with each trigger pull they were satisfied with an impacting bullet.

The more experienced Caleb was able to reload and fire three and four times faster than those armed with Hawkens but even then the overwhelming numbers of the Cheyenne were pushing to the bank of the river and appeared as if ready to cross. The three remaining vaqueros let loose another blast that temporarily halted those nearest the bank but as vaqueros stood to retreat as directed, the attackers pressed their advantage and splashed into the shallow waters of the stream. With the water flowing no deeper than waist high at the deepest, it did little to hinder their advance. Caleb and Jeremiah both turned their attention to those in the water and quickly dropped two warriors, Reuben also took aim and another dropped, only to be replaced by another. Colton and Chance were taking the measure of those still on the far bank but when they stopped to reload, Brewster saw one warrior rise from the near bank and he brought his Hawken to bear with his barrel dropping between the brothers and blasting the Indian back into the bloody water.

Caleb heard the signal from his father, a lingering wolf howl, to move back toward the cabins. Everyone had been told at that signal to fall back to the next firing line which would bring everyone closer together and make a more compact defense. Reuben rose and turned just as an arrow zipped to where he had been but it still creased his shoulder. Caleb saw the warrior trying to notch another arrow for a second attempt and with a quick turn he shouldered his Sharps and sent the warrior to meet his maker. He covered the fall back as the rest of the defenders moved to the second line of defense to assume their new positions. Reloading he found another target and let loose another messenger of death that stopped one of the apparent leaders of the mounted charge. He kept his position and loaded another paper cartridge and searched below to see if his men had moved and were prepared to continue the defense. He looked to the charging line of Cheyenne and noticed additional movement beyond. His heart stopped as he saw another wave of attackers, larger than the first, charging with an abandon and screaming their war cries while waving their lances in the air and shouting insults at those before them. Caleb knew his men were almost overwhelmed with those by the river and now with double that number in the coming wave, there would be no way to defend that attack. He left his position to join the others at the next line of defense and to warn them of the additional forces.

The first group of attackers, those charging on horseback, now neared the far bank of the river and were just about to start to cross when some of those in the rear shouted a warning. The leaders of the charge suddenly reined up and whirled their horses around and were startled to see another charge coming directly at them.

Before Caleb could reach his men, he turned to look again at the attackers when suddenly Reuben shouted, "It's Spotted Owl! Look! She brought her people!" Everyone stopped and stared as forty plus charging Ute shouted their war cries and waged their assault on the rear of the Cheyenne. The remaining attackers turned to face this new threat and those on foot on the near side of the river milled around in confusion and finally charged into the water to assist their brothers.

Caleb shouted to his men, "Come on, get your horses and follow me, we need to drive them outta here once and for all!" Their horses had been tethered in the edge of the clearing and tended by Little John. As they approached, he readily handed them off to the men and they quickly mounted and started after the fleeing Cheyenne. The attackers were trying to escape into the open plains but the Ute had anticipated their retreat and easily flanked their movement. The Ute bore down on them and the close quarter fight was one of blood for blood as the lances were used as the knights of old and the warriors rode down the fleeing quarry running them through and forcing the impaled enemy to the ground. Some of the Ute, so adept at riding, used their bows while guiding the horses at full gallop using only the pressure of their knees and sent arrow after arrow into their hated enemies. Others preferred the close in fighting and used their war axes or clubs and battered their opponent bloody or slashed them into gory pulp. By the time the ranch men had joined the Utes the fight was over, and the Ute warriors were shouting their victory cries and celebrating. Reuben and Owl were soon reunited and rejoicing together. Waters had returned to the cabin, but Caleb and Jeremiah joined the celebration to thank their friends and were introduced to Walkara and Lame Deer by a very proud Spotted Owl. "My father, this is Caleb, the leader of the village of the whites," she said, referring to Caleb, ". . .and this is his father, Jeremiah. Caleb is known among the Arapaho as He Who Talks to the Wind and his father is known as White Wolf."

"I am honored to meet the leader of the Ute people, and I am thankful for you joining in the battle," said Caleb with all due respect to the leader of the people.

"The Cheyenne have long been our enemy and to have a time to destroy some of our enemy is a good thing," then he smiled somewhat slyly, "and the Arapaho have also been our enemy, but no more. My daughter is a great warrior as well as a part of this village, so," waving his hands in resignation he continued, "I must keep my word and be at peace with her new family." He extended his arm as he smiled at Caleb and Jeremiah. "You would have been good enemies, you have fought well today."

"As have you," added Jeremiah as the men clasped forearms in a traditional greeting.

The celebration was brief by the standards of any native people but the real celebration would take place after the return to the village. The good-byes were brief and promises were made to visit each other's village and the Utes began their return trek. Caleb was anxious to get back to the cabin and see his new son and check on his wife. He looked at his father and asked, "Did anybody else get hurt during the fight?"

"I think the only thing was a couple flesh wounds from arrows, but nothing real serious. Reuben got a crease on his shoulder and Chance got stuck with an arrow but I don't think it's bad," answered Jeremiah with a bit of a grin that Caleb didn't notice.

The men turned the horses into the corral and hung up the tack and saddles and walked to the steps to mount the porch and enter the cabin. They were anxiously looking forward to a good meal and some hot coffee, knowing the big task of clearing the flats of the remains of the attack would take most of the day and it was not a job they were anxious to begin. As they entered the cabin, Caleb saw Waters sitting in the rocking chair and holding a bundle that he knew to be his son. He walked over to her to look at the boy and pushed the blanket aside to see the wrinkled face that was snuggled up in sleep. He smiled at the child and at his Ma and quietly asked, "Is Clancy O.K.?'

"She is fine, she's waiting on you. Go see her," instructed Waters.

Caleb quietly pushed open the door to the bedroom and saw the smiling face of his wife and she motioned him in with a wave of her hand. He stood tall and smiled as he stepped to her side and she patted the edge of the bed for him to sit down. As he was seated, she asked, "Do you want to hold your son?" and leaned forward extending her arms with a bundled blanket before her. Caleb looked at her and at the bundle before him, smiled and looked at the face of his son and cradled him in his arms and said, "He sure is a fine looking boy . . ." a frown crossed his face and he looked back at the closed door, then at Clancy and with his free hand he pointed to the door and looked back at a smiling Clancy as she slowly held up her hand and curled her fingers leaving two upright and started giggling.

"You mean . . .two . . . twins? Really? Twins?" He

jumped to his feet almost dropping the child he held in his arms and looked down at Clancy and bent over to kiss and hug his giggling wife and stood again and spun around not knowing what to do and shouted, "TWINS!" resulting in a startled baby that let out a squall almost as loud as his father.

CHANCE THREET HUNG BETWEEN COLTON AND Brewster with Marylyn anxiously following behind cautioning the two to be careful with their burden. With their arms intertwined over their shoulders, the two men were walking toward the porch and cautiously picking their steps so as not to cause Chance any undo agony. However, the expressions on their faces did not match the caution as commanded by the distraught Marylyn while she continuously scolded the burden bearers. "Be careful, you're hurting him!" while the only response from Chance was oft repeated moans and facial expressions that told of agonizing pain. As they reached the top of the steps she hollered, "Don't sit him down, he can't sit! Take him inside!"

As they pushed through the door, the women were surprised to see another wounded man that would require their attention. They noted his bloody trousers leg and Mrs. Sparger motioned for the men to seat him at the table but Marylyn corrected, "No, lay him on the floor, there, in front of the fire." As the men maneuvered to lay Chance down, everyone in the room had to catch themselves to keep from laughing. He was indeed wounded and it was a serious wound, but to see the feathered arrow protruding from his posterior was just a touch on the funny side. To add to the humor was the attention heaped upon him by the young woman, Marylyn. She was determined to be the one that tended to his injury and it didn't matter if it was proper or not, she wasn't concerned about propriety but only about the welfare of this man that had become so important to her.

"Well, ladies, since we won't be much help with his uh . . .wound . . .would it be alright if we had us a cup of coffee?" asked Colton as he struggled to keep from snickering at his brother's consternation. Chance was now stretched out on his stomach and propped on his elbows looking up at his brother and the rest of the onlookers with an expression that told of his irritation with their attitude more than discomfort from the wound.

"Go ahead and laugh. But just you wait, next time one of you need help with fightin' injuns or takin' on a grizz' or some wolves, I'm just gonna sit back an' laugh. Just wait, you'll see."

His remark was like opening the floodgates to the pent up laughter that everyone had been holding and the tension that had built up from the battle and the birthing was suddenly and happily relieved.

Caleb, still holding one of his sons, looked down at the wounded man and said, "Well, Chance, it looks like you're gonna need considerable tendin' to, what with not bein' able to sit a horse, or walk around much, or hardly anythin' else, now who do you s'pose we can get to nurse you along?" he chuckled as he looked at Marylyn who was now seated on the floor beside her patient. She looked up at Caleb and said, "I'm thinkin' this might be a good time to teach this boy some manners, and maybe a few other things about bein' the right kind of cowboy, whatcha think Mr. C?"

"You know, Marylyn, you might be right about that. Course, I can't see him bein' able to throw a loop, or sit a saddle, or much of anything like that. But I reckon you can find somethin' to teach him. Whatchu think Chance?"

The only answer that came from the floor was "How 'bout gettin' this arrow out before you start plannin' my future?"

After clearing the room, Caleb to the bedroom and the rest of the men to the porch, Mrs. Sparger and Marylyn went to work on the wound of Chance. Nurse Sparger had arrayed the doctor's tools on a clean cloth to the side, each one carefully cleaned with the medicinal whiskey the doctor always kept in his bag, and explained to Marylyn and Chance what they would be doing. "Now Chance, this is going to be very painful, I've given you that knife scabbard for you to bite down on and that'll help a little. You'll probably pass out from the pain, but I'm sure you'll be O.K. Now, are you ready?" Chance mumbled and nodded his head for her to start.

Her first action was to cut most of the shaft off so it would not hinder their work, and then she began carefully enlarging the entrance of the wound to enable the removal of the rest of the arrow. It was a difficult and laborious procedure and Chance would tense his muscles, relax to take a deep breath, tense again and that made the cutting even more challenging. Finally she noticed the muscles relax and she knew he had passed out. She quickly and efficiently cut to the depth of the arrowhead and slowly removed the rest of the arrow intact. After examining the wound, she rinsed it with the whiskey and washed the surface and with some catgut sewed the cut together and covered it with a fresh bandage. She sat back and looked at Marylyn and both women smiled with approval knowing their patient would recover satisfactorily.

The men's cabin had been turned into a recovery hospital with Diego Martinez and Chance Threet as the patients. Both Colton Threet and Brewster still bunked there, but Marylyn spent most of the daylight hours tending to the patients. Diego was able to be up and about and was mending well so most of the time during the day, the only patient was the prone form of Chance Threet lying on his stomach with Marylyn sitting on the edge of the bed tending to his needs. Occasionally he was able to get up and walk, but even that was painful and seldom done except when absolutely necessary. But that gave Marylyn ample excuse to spend more time at his side. They shared stories of their lives before the Medicine Bow and found many parallels that gave common ground and understanding. The more time spent together the closer they became to one another.

She walked beside him with her arm around his waist to give him some stability and he had his arm on her shoulders. It was their first walk together just to be out of the cabin.

"You know, from the first time I saw you, when you were crackin' that whip over them horses, I thought you were pretty special and then when I saw how pretty you was, well, I was kinda taken with you right off," he said as he bashfully dropped his head.

"Me too," replied Marylyn, somewhat boldly.

"You too, what? Whatchu mean?" asked Chance.

"I was taken with you right off too, I've never felt like that before and I didn't rightly know what to do, but after you flattened Ashton, I knew then that you were the one for me."

"Really?" responded Chance hopefully.

"Well, good night, Chance, you think I been hangin' around here these last few days for nothin'?"

He pulled her to him and held her tightly. She pulled back and lifted her face up to his and he eagerly met her lips with his as they shared their first kiss. As they pulled back to look at one another, broad smiles painted their faces and they kissed again, only to be interrupted by Colton as he said, "Hey you two, cut that out. You shouldn't be doin' that in front of us children." Brewster joined him as they laughed together with knowing smiles.

"So, does this mean you'll be able to walk to the main cabin for the meals and she won't have to cater to you at our cabin?"

"Yeah, I s'pose so, but don't go 'spectin me to be ridin' no horses for a spell yet. You're gonna haveta' take care of that for a while," cautioned Chance to his brother.

With effort, Chance and Marylyn negotiated the

stairs and entered the cabin to the surprise of the ladies that were busy with the noon meal preparations. The two Barbaras turned and clapped their hands together when they saw the couple make it to the table and Chance be seated, rather gingerly and on one side, while Marylyn assisted. It had been evident for some time what was happening between the two young people and the two romantics called Barbara looked at one another and smiled. As they nodded their heads to one another they turned back to the task of preparing the meal.

Clancy came from the bedroom with one child bundled in her arm and seated herself as she asked Mary-lyn, "Could you please bring Talon to me? He's still on the bed," she motioned to the bedroom. Chance asked, "So, you've named them?" looking at the one she was holding and preparing to nurse, "and what's this one's handle?"

"This one is Tyrell. Tyrell and Talon, we never thought we'd have twins, but Barbara said she knew after she first examined me but didn't want to alarm me. After she heard about our first loss she didn't think I needed anything more to worry about, so they were a surprise even to me." As she finished speaking she looked down at the babe that was enthusiastically nursing and then accepted the second boy and with the aid of Marylyn was soon doing double duty. Chance had turned away and was dutifully nursing his cup of coffee as he let his mind wander with thoughts of his future and the possibility of building a life with Marylyn.

Life on the frontier was uncertain at best and chal-lenges were too many to count and most of the pioneers knew to take advantage of every opportunity that was given. Chance knew he was a part of building something special here in the Medicine Bow valley and he liked the idea of being a part of a ranch and with Marylyn at his side he thought they would make a good team and maybe someday could build a ranch of their own. He pictured the two of them with their own cabin and ranch with lots of cattle and maybe even a couple of boys to help, but not redheaded freckle faced ones like the twins, he grinned. Then looking at Marylyn as she watched Clancy and he knew that with both of them having blonde hair and fair complexions, their kids would be just like them, tow heads and light skinned. He smiled at the thought and Marylyn looked at him and asked, "Now what's got you to smiling so big?"

"Ah, nothin', just thinkin'," he mumbled.

"Dear, would you please call the rest of the men in to eat?" asked Barbara Brown of Marylyn. The young woman smiled and rose to go to the porch and summon the others. Clancy was still in the rocking chair with the babies but they were under a light blanket and would soon be drifting off for their nap but Caleb had to have a peek at his sons and walked to her side and pulled the blanket back to look at his boys. "Yup, every time I look at 'em it seems like their hair gets redder and their freckles multiply," and smiled up at his redhead beauty.

She reached up and pulled his head down to hers and gave him a long kiss and as they pulled apart, she said, "Your favorite flavor is strawberry anyway, isn't it?"

"Yes m'am, sure 'nuff," he knew it wouldn't do to contradict his favorite wife on something as touchy as strawberry versus chocolate so he left well enough alone. She handed one of the boys to her husband and nodded for him to take the child to the bedroom and she followed after carrying the other.

Reuben and Spotted Owl were absent from the noon meal as Owl wanted to prepare the meals for her husband and use the time to continue to work on their home. This was the first time for her to live in a cabin, although it was not a big change from the wickiup, but she wanted it to be their home and that meant making the little changes to become theirs. In the white man's world a woman would call it decorating, but for Owl it was 'making the spirits welcome'. As such, the interior of their home held the decorations of war shields, lances, hand woven baskets and blankets, tanned hides and robes and more. Reuben's only concern was comfort and Owl certainly made their home comfortable for the two of them.

Reuben and Owl were both involved in the daily activities of the ranch with moving cattle, cutting grass for the winter, and finding and eliminating any hazards to the animals. Owl preferred the hunting trips and curing the hides and other preparations for winter that she was more accustomed to but those duties were shared by everyone. However, when Caleb spoke of mustangs, she quickly volunteered to scout out the herd of mustangs so she and Reuben were given that responsibility exclusively.

"There, coming out of that draw, see?" asked Owl as she pointed to the far ravine across the narrow valley. Reuben shaded his eyes and looked in the direction of her point and waited. What first appeared as a shadow began to move, then as he watched a herd of more than twenty mustangs trailed out of the ravine into the valley. The stream that meandered through the grassy valley beckoned the animals and they lined out along the bank with a couple wading into the water. A couple of yearlings and one spritely colt played in the shallow water while the mares kept watch. Behind them was a tall muscled and scarred stallion that was the herd boss and he patrolled the bunch with authority.

"There's some good lookin' animals in that bunch," said Reuben as he and Owl sat astride their horses. They were shielded from view by a cluster of juniper as they watched from the slight hillside. "But I don't know if Caleb will be wantin' us to do anythin' but just keep an eye on 'em."

"With winter coming, it would be best to let them be. If we captured them, we would have to feed them and break them in the winter time and that would be hard. Best to wait until Spring," stated Owl.

Reuben looked at his wife and smiled, "You know, I never thought of that, but that would be the smart thing to do. Let's go back to the ranch and let Caleb know what we found."

It was late afternoon when Reuben and Owl rode back into the clearing at the main cabin and found Caleb and Clancy on the porch, watching the grandparents, Jeremiah and Waters sitting with babes in arms. Reuben sat with arms folded on the saddle horn as Owl sat erect and watched, "We found a good herd of mustangs, over cross the valley near the top end o' the Sierra Madre.

There was o'er twenty head and a few young ones and some o' the mares looked like they might be carryin'."

"That sounds good. Do ya think it'll be hard to round 'em up?" asked Caleb.

"Nah, but Owl had a pretty good idea and I'm thinkin' she's probably right," drolled Reuben.

"What's that?"

"If we let 'em be till Spring, we won't have to feed 'em thru the winter and it'll be too cold and snowy to mess with 'em anyway, so just wait for fair weather then round 'em up."

Caleb gave it some thought, looked at Jeremiah and saw by his expression he agreed, and said to Reuben, "That sounds like the smart thing to do. We've got enough animals to be concerned about already. Well, put your horses up and join us for supper. This is the last meal with my folks here, they're leavin' in the morning and it'd be a good time to share."

Reuben looked to Owl and received a knowing and agreeing smile and with a tip of his hat to everyone on the porch said, "Sounds good, we'll be back in a bit."

There were just too many people to have a sit down dinner in the house so Waters took charge and decided to have the meal prepared and shared outside. The cook fire had a large metal rotisserie with a hind quarter of an elk sizzling over the flames and two big dutch ovens were hidden under the hot grey coals at the side. Opposite the dutch ovens stood a large tripod that held a big pot with a lid and a large enamel coffee pot sat on a flat stone at the edge of the fire. The women, Waters, Owl, Clancy and Marylyn tended the doin's giving the two Barbaras a chance to sit and hold the babies. The men had put together a game of horseshoes and were busy throwing and laughing as each one took his turn. Little John was getting the best of all the others much to the dismay of Jackson Bubash who had previously bragged about his skills. It was a good time and everyone thoroughly enjoyed themselves and when the sunset cast its skirt of gold across the entire horizon, they joined hands and thanked God for his bounty and blessings.

"WELL IT LOOKS LIKE WE'RE GONNA BE BUILDIN' some more cabins," said Caleb as he lay with his hands behind his head and looking at Clancy. She was on her side with her hands tucked under the pillow as she looked at her husband and said, "And what makes you say that?"

"Well, the ladies," meaning the two Barbaras, ". . .asked me today if it'd be all right for them to stay on here and make this their home. They offered to help any way they could, you know cookin' and such for the crew or what have you, just about anything."

"And what did you tell them?"

"Well I told 'em sure they could, what'd you 'spect me to say?" he said as he grinned at her. "I mean, after all, they're practically family and it's been good havin' someone that can do all the doctorin' we needed."

"Ummhumm, and have you noticed the way Jackson keeps hanging around? I'm not sure which one he has his eye on, but I wouldn't be surprised if he . . ."

"You don't mean, why that ole' coot. Hummmm, lemme see . . ."

"What are you thinkin' now?" asked Clancy.

"Well, I was thinkin' we'd have to build a cabin for the ladies, and I was thinkin' 'bout, well, buildin' another one. What I was thinkin' was we'd say it was for Jackson and his daughter but probably by the time we got it finished, it would be for Marylyn and Chance instead."

Clancy giggled, "Well at least you're not totally blind. I was beginning to wonder if you knew they were sweet on each other or not."

He looked at her and continued thinking, "And then we can have Jackson move in with Colton and Brewster. But if Jackson moves too soon, we'll have to build one for him and whichever Barbara he ends up with."

"I don't think that'll happen anytime soon, neither one of those ladies are as interested as he is and they all just like flirtin' is all I'm thinkin'" observed Clancy. She frowned as she thought, "What about the vaqueros, what if they decide to stay?"

"No, they're headin' out in the mornin' too. They'll ride a ways with Ma and Pa but they'll keep on goin' to California. They figgered if they wait any longer it'll be into winter and then they'd have to wait till next year, so they're goin' on out. It seems they got family that's expectin' 'em. I told 'em they'd be welcome to stay, but they've got commitments so . . ."

"Well, let's try to get some sleep before the twins decide to wake us up again."

"Good idea," he said and kissed his wife before rolling over and quickly falling asleep. Clancy just shook her head as she lay awake waiting for the stirring of the twins to call her back to duty.

The men's cabin was also filled with bedside conversation as Colton grilled Chance about his intentions with Marylyn. "So, you think the two of you are gonna be gettin' married?"

"Married? Whatever gave you that idea?" replied Chance.

"Well the way you been sparkin' her, and the way the two of you look at each other, ever'body figgers that's whatchu got on your mind."

"Oh they do, do they?" asked Chance.

"Well, don'tchu?"

He fell silent for a few moments as he let his mind dwell on the girl and he let a smile stretch his face, knowing the others couldn't see it in the dark. "Well, we have talked about it a little, but don't say anything, cuz we ain't said nuthin' to her Pa."

There were chuckles all around as the men knew the nervous emotions that were stirred whenever a courting young man thought of a girl's father. Brewster piped up with, "If we was still in the city, you could just do what they call elope, you know, just run off an' get married."

"Ain't no place to run off to! But come to think of it, how could we get married anyway, ain't nobody around that could do it. I mean we ain't got no preacher or nuthin'," said Chance.

"What'd Reuben do? Didn't he marry Spotted Owl?" asked Colton.

"Yeah, but with the Utes, the Chief is the one that does all that and when Reuben and Owl went to him, Reuben said all the Chief done is said, 'you're hitched' and that was it," said Brewster. "But I don't think the Chief would do it for you cuz you ain't Ute."

"Oh well, we'll just have to figger somethin' else out, I reckon," groaned Chance as he turned over to go to sleep.

The vaqueros, more experienced with life and love, chuckled among themselves at the young men and their thoughts about romance and marriage.

Breakfast was a silent affair as the group ate in shifts. The younger men were first at the table and dismissed themselves to get the horses ready for Jeremiah and Waters and to help the vaqueros pack up. Caleb and Clancy sat with Jeremiah and Waters and shared thoughts and remembrances. "Be sure to give Pine Leaf a big hug for me, please," asked Clancy as she looked at Waters. "I still remember that first hunt we went on together, I was so afraid of her, but she became such a good friend and I grew to love her."

"She always ask me about you. She and Shield now have two children and they are going to have another," answered Waters with a smile.

"Oh my, that's wonderful. I'm happy for her. Well, she was a war leader and now she'll have her own war party," laughed Clancy.

Jeremiah and Caleb walked to the door and Jeremiah cradled his new Sharps in his arm as he said, "I sure do like the way this thing shoots, it's everything they said it was, that's for sure. Thanks son." They walked together to the horses tethered at the corrals. Jeremiah carefully checked the riggings on both horses, then on the pack horse and stepping to the side of Little John he asked, "You check everything on your horse son?"

"You know I did, Pa, I always do."

"I know, but you can never be too careful, remember that," said Jeremiah, always the teaching father.

Clancy and Waters waited on the porch and almost unnoticed the clearing began to fill up with all the members of the growing settlement. The vaqueros rode their horses into the clearing but sat patiently to the side. Reuben and Spotted Owl walked up the path from their cabin, intercepting Jackson and Marylyn on the way. The Threet brothers and Brewster, having finished their favor of readying the mounts, now walked back to the side of the porch and stood silently waiting.

Waters slipped a foot into the stirrup and swung gracefully astride her horse to join her husband and the two looked down at Jeremiah and Clancy standing arm in arm by the horses. Caleb put one hand on the mane of Jeremiah's horse and asked his Pa, "Could we have a prayer before you go?"

"Sure son, that'd be fine."

Caleb began with "Our Heavenly Father, we are so thankful we've had this time together and we're thankful for your protecting hand upon us . . ." everyone bowed their heads and the men had removed their hats as Caleb continued in his prayer of thanksgiving and pleading for God's care. When he concluded with an "Amen" others echoed his word and all looked to the gathering at the center of the clearing. Caleb shook his Pa's hand and Waters and Clancy clasped hands and good byes were said with tears in every eye present.

Jeremiah reined his mount around and followed by Waters and Little John leading the pack horse, the vaqueros trailing along after, the group walked their horses down the trail to the river crossing while the remainder gathered together to watch them all the way. After they waded the river, they turned to give another wave that was answered by the extended arms of the cluster in the clearing and the riders soon disappeared in the distance.

To break the somber mood, Caleb said, "Well folks, we've got our work cut out for us. We've got two more cabins to build!"

Everyone stopped at looked at him as he continued, "Yup, the ladies have decided to become a part of our little community," as he motioned toward the two Barbaras, ". . . and I'm sure ol' Jackson and his daughter would rather have a cabin instead of a teepee come winter time, so we better get to buildin'!"

Chance and Marylyn just happened to be standing together with arms around each other and looked to one another and with a gentle squeeze smiled knowingly.

———

End

When a marauding band of Cheyenne Dog Soldiers attack a wagon train and take two women and a boy captive, Talon Thompsett is surprised when no one is willing to go after the Indians and try to rescue the captives. But the young man is reminded of his father's counsel that "Whenever a task falls to you, don't question the why of it, just get busy with the doin' of it!" Now he must set aside his new job as Shotgun for the Overland Stage and gear up for the pursuit of a band of warrior renegades. A tall task for an unproven young man, but when none of the pilgrims believe in the cause, and the settlers of nearby LaPorte refuse to leave their homes unguarded, Talon realizes he must face this challenge alone. His commitment and determination lead to the making of a man and a bloody chase through the foothills of Colorado and the plains of the new territory. Along the way, he makes a bitter enemy of the Cheyenne war leader, Two Bears, who is determined to seek vengeance on this unknown white man and prove to his people that he is the chosen leader of the notorious Dog soldiers. But Talon is undaunted and even eager to show the renegade that this white man is more than his match. Follow the trail that takes a young man from the Cache La Poudre through intimidating country and back to the Overland Trail as he proves his worth as he rises to the challenge and the making of a man.

AVAILABLE NOW FROM B.N. RUNDELL AND WOLFPACK PUBLISHING